Drumming After Dark

Short Stories and Poems About Romance and Fantasy

By Vachon Hastings

Contents

Preface

History enlightens us to the complexities of love, lust, and sex. The Bible documented the lustful sins performed by the most revered, and the disciples of Jesus pontificated about infidelity and sexual immorality, but the physical desires of the past are just as prevalent today.

After watching many episodes of PBS's "Finding Your Roots," I've concluded that despite race, creed, nationality or gender, human beings are looking for love or a lustful moment. which is why in nearly every episode, there's a revelation that someone's presumed father or grandfather is of no DNA relation, or their paternal ancestor fathered other children outside his home.

Sex itself is not immoral. It is as natural to humans as it is to canines. It is how we, as people, express love, disappointment, trauma, and peace—and it's also how we heal. Whether acted upon or not, and whether it is in the comfort and security of our bedrooms, in a monogamous relationship, or embedded in our private thoughts—and even if we choose celibacy—intimacy and sex is inherent to our human construct.

This book is a compilation of poems and short stories in the romance and romantasy genres, which will enable you to meet characters who experience love, loss, the duality of self, and the sexual exposés that are an integral part of their story. Each of these stories will allow the reader to embark on a different adventure.

The Beginning

Not a day goes by when I don't think of you. Longing to recapture the moments that we shared. Feelings of regret nag at my heart. I regret that I never uttered the words "I love you" to you orally and physically. My emotions hidden in the shadows of apprehension and broken confidence. I fell in love with you at first sight, at the slight tug of my arm with your brawny hands, and that deviously sexy smile that secretly made me feel like a schoolgirl. Amused by your wit. Struck by your intelligence. Warmed by your softness. Yet, I hid. Fearful of the possibility of a love so strong. I hid. Stoic and steadfast in my display of affection. I often ponder the times when we laid unclothed, skin to skin, sleeping peacefully, and you would gently pull the covers up when you exited the bed to ensure I stayed cozy and warm. MMM, the thoughtfulness still makes my heart happy.

I miss holding your strong arms during our moments of passion, while you gently engaged my moist cavity with your large, masculine stick. The lovemaking was good. I wanted to do more. I hid. I have regrets, but I am also thankful for your friendship. Thank you for unknowingly teaching me to no longer hide, and to speak my love and affection with my words, my body, and my presence. You taught me how to show and accept love. I hide no more. I revealed my inner feelings of passion to my new love.

In still moments, I stare out, visualizing you as the father of my children, my mate. Pondering what "family" would look like in our world together. Me, listening to your stories while you cook your favorite meals with the dishtowel haphazardly thrown over your shoulder. You, swaying your head back and laughing at my silly stories, as we pendulate the lightly humorous conversation.

A far away dream.

Your touch is still present on my spine. I can still feel the weight of your hand pressing down on me with softness and coital intensity, massaging my torso and caressing my breast with loving firmness. I can feel you gently wrapping your lips around each nipple, slowly suckling. Your hand presses lightly on my neck. I sink fully into submission. Encapsulated by lust, I receive you. There is a slow, intentional undulation of our bodies. Then we rest for the night, and, as is customary, your early morning departure leaves me quietly panged.

I hid.

I will always hold a place for you in my heart.

My song for us: Tracie Chapman, "The Promise"

Love Slave: Stone

"We are birthed from the womb with the desire to be loved, and some will seek it amongst the shadows, but love embraced in darkness will be consumed by darkness."
—Vachon

"Did ya say somethin gal? Best suits you better to get those sacs filled fore' sundown. So, hush yo mouths and git busy!" brutely shouted Mr. Little, the Master's younger brother.

I's did just that. I labored so hard, so long, the sun was 'bout down, and the moon's light was distant. My back hurt something fierce, and my hands and fingertips were cracked with little speckles of blood on them, but I picked that cotton without falter, so help me God. 'Bout time I's got back to my cabin; I was dog-tired. I had no shoes, and my clothes were tattered—bad enough they's was made from linen scraps, but we field workers made do. I shared my one-room cabin with Sally. Sally was new here. She was from some farm near Virginia, where she said that she once had a whole family: a husband and two children—a boy and a girl. The Master died, she said, and the wife didn't want to manage all the slaves, so she sold them off. She didn't talk much, which was quite suitable for me. Sometimes, folk talk too much, but I think she didn't talk a lot cause she was sad. She missed her family. She was a hard worker, too. She just kept her head down, while her hands and feet kept moving.

In our cabin, there was a small wash basin with a bar of lye soap lying next to it, infused with oil from the wildflowers I picked. The soap smelled *so* good. Some of the other workers asked me why I always smelled so good. I let that be's my little secret. It was the combination of the flowers I used, and I wasn't givin' up my recipe.

I's washed myself up as best I could—and quickly, 'cause I had some burning questions to ask Sally. I plopped down next to her outside on the small, gray, wooden front porch. It was dark, and the moon stood tall, delivering a peaceful light. Usually, there wasn't much peace to be seen around here. It was a quiet night.

"What's it like?" I asked.

"What's what like?" she inquired, with a look of confusion.

"Havin a family, and a husband and children? What's it like?"

"Stone, it don't matter now, do it?" questioned Sally in a rich, deep, sullen tone. "I ain't got none of them here with me. I don't know where my children are. How you gon' ask me a question like that?"

"Ah, I'm sorry. Don't mean to upset you. It's just that I dream of havin' my own family sometime—even if it's only for a short while," I noted. "Havin' a husband to laugh with and talk to and tell my deepest thoughts to… I's dreams of that, and making babies. I wanna have my own children one day. I want to love someone. I'm sorry about what happened to your family, Sally. I really am. I knows that's why you always so sad. My momma died some time ago, and I never knew my daddy, but my momma says he was a real nice guy—and soft on da eyes, too."

"He used to rub pork salve on my hands at night, 'cause they would be hurting after working da crops all day," said Sally. "He made me feel special, and he was always tellin' these wild stories, and our children would be listenin' real good to his stories. He was a good daddy—and good in bed, too," she snickered. "I miss him so. I miss my babies, too."

"Well, Moses been talking real sweet to me," I said coyly. "He always looking at me with soft eyes."

"That's how it begins. A man should like you more than you like him. He needs to come for you," explained Sally, as she stood and gathered her linen dress to go back inside and prepare for bed. "Goodnight," she said.

"Night," I replied.

Early the next morning, I woke gasping to the sound of footsteps outside our cabin door. We gets nervous when folks make unexpected visits at wayward hours of the day 'cause it's often not good news. I rolled so fast out of my hard wood bed that I didn't even notice how cold the room was. I slowly opened the heavy wood-framed door—only to find a large piece of warm bread and butter, wrapped in paper, lying on my front porch. As I bent down to fetch it, I looked up and caught Moses in his tattered, stained linens, standing near the next cabin, watching with a slight smile.

It was him. He brought me the bread and butter, and I'm not sure how he got hold of it, but I sweetly smiled back at him, showing that I approved, and I was grateful. My heart almost burst with excitement and wondrous joy. He liked me! Moses was doin' just like Sally said he should. He was coming for me!

As I turned to walk back into the cabin, I looked back, and Moses was still there, like he was on duty, but I thought I saw his eyes turn a bright yellow. Strange. It must have been the morning sun shining on him, because only a man that handsome could take on the sun's rays like that. He was tall and muscular, with deep brown skin. He had a strong jaw and nose, and sweet eyes. He was handsome.

It was Saturday, and Sundays were our day of rest, which meant Saturday nights were meant for fun. We built a fire at dark and rolled plenty of logs to sit on around the fire. Some of the men cooked meat over the wood fire on large iron grates, and the women brought whatever food we could prepare—mostly from our own gardens—to go nicely with the meat. I, myself, brought cooked peas with a little pork fat and onion. Abraham, another field hand, brought some of the moonshine he made. I don't know when he found the time 'cause that was enough to supply two plantations. Moses wasn't there to help. I's assumed that maybe he was just tired from a long workday. He was so tall and muscular; Moses often got asked to help with a lot of heavy movin' and extra duties, so perhaps he was just tired.

We had ourselves a good time, laughin', singin', dancin', and eatin'. I drank my share of Abraham's moonshine, which I called "good time," 'cause you drank that, and you was gon' have a good time. As I sat 'round the fire, laughing, I looked up and saw Moses quietly standing a ways off to the side, leaning on one of the trees. He was staring my way. Some of the others sitting around caught the direction of my eyes, then turned and followed them to Moses.

"Ah, I see you got eyes for Moses," said Coffey, one of other field hands.

The men began to softly chatter amongst the group.

"Anyone know anything about him?"

"He don't talk much to nobody—cept' for Stone. Seems he's taken a likin' to our Stone here."

"He just showed up one day. Even Massa Little didn't know where he came from, but he could use the help, and nobody reported a missing slave."

"Yeah, sometimes he does strange stuff, like strange ways of movin' his body. I can't 'splain it."

"Y'all so full of nonsense. You fools just jealous you ain't that handsome and strong," I interjected.

My eyes were still fixed on Moses; I saw him signal me to come to him. I rose, but I desperately tried not to appear too excited, so I took my time as I walked in his direction, but I was as giddy as a child getting the first piece of warm cake.

"You havin a good time?" asked Moses.

"Yeah, havin' myself a real good time. The food's real good, and Ismeal did a good job smokin' the meat. It's tender and full of flavor. Why you ain't over there with the rest of us?" I asked.

"It was a long day, and I was just tired. Didn't really feel up to much company, but I's not too tired to talk to you, and you smell good, like fresh flowers. Real pretty," acknowledged Moses.

"Thank you. I make it myself," I told him. "Is this your cabin right here?" I pointed.

Moses stuck his hands in his pockets, re-situated himself against the tree, and cooly nodded. "Yeah, it's not much, but ya welcome to come in a take a peek. I don't share it with nobody."

I nodded in agreement.

Moses was right. His cabin wasn't much at all: a water jug, a straw mattress, a basket with a few food items, and some threads thrown across a makeshift chair. Not much at all, but at least his floors were made of wood.

Moses stepped close to me. I could almost feel his breath. "Can I fetch you some water?" asked Moses in a quiet, deep tone.

"I'm fine. Thank you," I replied.

There was silence, but it was the loudest silence I ever felt. The vibrations between us were deafening.

His rock-hard body was pulsating, so I could hear his heartbeat, and I was certain he could hear mine.

We stood there, admiring one another intensely, focused. Our eyes fixed on each other. Warmth came over my body, and my bosoms became firm and sensitive. I never craved a man like I craved him in that moment. Moses wrapped his arms around my waist, firm and strong, and we began to kiss. His lips were large and soft. I sank deep into his embrace. There was a scent coming from his body that was intoxicating. With every inhale, I felt like I had drunk more of that moonshine. I'm not sure how that was possible, and I wasn't askin' no questions at that time.

Moses picked me up and then laid me on his thin straw-stuffed mattress. He knelt in front of me and undressed himself, removing his shirt and then his pants. I didn't know a man's parts could be so large. I thought for a second *I could hang a towel on that thing*! He moved in and straddled me. Raised my arms above my head and pulled my dress up over my body.

Naked.

That smell was there again. It was a mixture of musk, flowers, and something else I couldn't name, but it had me. He began to fondle my bosoms, licking and sucking them. At times, it felt a bit rough, but I wanted more. He slid down towards my hips, spread my legs wide, and began nibbling on my inner thighs.

I ran my hands down the upper portion of his back. *What am I feeling?* There were small, raised bumps on his back, with sharp tips that penetrated his skin. Maybe he got whipped, and that was how his skin healed.

I didn't want him to stop. The small nibbling became intense tongue strokes on my lady parts, and occasionally I felt a sharp nibble. My body was respondin' immensely. I began to quiver. Moses rose on top of me and inserted himself. Wetness was running down my leg. He was moving in hard, fast strokes, pounding over and over again. His eyes… they flickered yellow again. I couldn't move. I wanted everything he had to give. He was pounding up, down, and side to side, all the way out and back in again. *Pounding.*

Moses lifted his chest all the way up, and a soft growl accompanied his yellow eyes. I didn't know what to make of it. My juices were still flowing.

Don't stop.

The growl grew louder. Moses tilted his head back and became rigid. I could see every muscle in his body, and it looked like they were growing bigger. Large, dark wings spread from his back, like a demon angel from the Bible that the preacher said about on Sunday mornings.

Pounding.

The beating of drums reverberated through the room, like the drumming we danced to late at night. It was fast and low.

Boom, boom, boom, boom, boom.

I began to throb again, and I couldn't control it. I didn't want to control it. It felt so good. I could feel the wetness under my thighs, but it was like our bodies became one. He looked deep into my soul. His yellow eyes piercing at me and he opened his mouth wide. I could see his fangs, and he asked me, "Do you take me?"

"YES!" I whispered heavily.

He pressed his body down on me. He was still pounding, and rhythmically moving his body.

He drove his fangs gently into my neck. His magic ejected into my veins, and I could feel its electric fire moving through me. Moses stiffened, hummed a deep growl, and released his seed inside me.

Boom, boom, boom, boom, boom.

The drumming echoed through the room. When I awakened, Moses was gone. He had left the cabin and was missing from the plantation all together.

10 Months Later

The flappin' from the wings of the bird flyin' high in the sky echoes loudly in my ears. Field workers chattering clean across the field are as clear as the person kneeling next to me humming an old hymn. For months, the pain was nearly intolerable. My body hurt all over and I was always sweatin'. No one took much notice because everyone's body around here hurt from the kind of work that we do. But now, the pain is gon'. I've been reborn and gifted with new life.

"Stone!" called Sally. "That's an awful pretty baby, but I've never seen a baby eat so much—and I've been meaning to ask if you feelin' okay? It kinda sounds like you growling at night, like one of those old crazy stories my husband used to tell—but I know better than for that mess to be true."

I looked away and smirked. "I've neva felt better."

Luna

"It is the flesh that has been abandoned, devoid of pleasure—
even in the presence of spiritual delight."
—Vachon

It had been three days since I first witnessed the power of quiet. The kids departed to the in-laws for two weeks for part of their summer break and Nate was out of state on travel for his job for eight full days. I welcomed the quiet and the stillness. Silence. To capture the fullness of the unobtrusive period, I scheduled myself to work half-days during this time. Takeout once a day, water and martinis quickly became my new daily menu. I didn't wash a single dish and rather chose to rinse and reuse my martini glass to garnish my next drink. On one of my bartending expeditions in my kitchen, I noticed a raunchy smell coming from the sink. To my dismay, I flipped on the switch to the disposal, and it didn't start.

I texted Nate:

Me: "Hey, babe, I know you're probably working. Don't mean to disturb you, but the disposal is not working, and I think there's food stuck in it, and it's starting to smell pretty rank. What do you want me to do?"

Nate: "Hey hun, no problem. We're on a short break anyways. I think Vic next door is home. Let me text him and see if he can walk over and take a look at it."

Me: "Thanks."

Nate: "He said it's cool. He'll be there in 10."

Vic arrived at my front door in eight minutes, holding a toolbox in his left hand. He was dressed as if he were either on his way to the gym to work out, or he had just left the gym. He wore knee-length gym shorts, a loose-fitting t-shirt that barely showed the outline of his six-pack abs, an athletic watch, and clean sneakers on his "6'2" inch, 225-pound bronzed frame. I knew my way around a man's build, and I was certain he was two-twenty-five, give or take a few pounds. When I opened the door, I greeted him almost professionally, as if he were an Amazon delivery guy, and I did my damnedest not to stare at his rock-hard body, chiseled face, full lips, and straight teeth. He was a lickable sight to see. I desperately tried to avoid sensually biting my lip with lustful intentions. Damn, he was sexy.

I never really took notice of Vic before. He and his wife Carrie had lived next door to us for the last eight years, but I hadn't seen much of Carrie lately. Carrie and I had spoken casually on several occasions, but it never developed into a deeper friendship. Nate and Vic would often sit in the yard, share a beer, and talk.

I led Vic to the kitchen and expressively told him about the issue with the disposal. It was more like a Vanna White performance. He gently placed the plastic toolbox down on the tiled floors, opened the cabinet doors, and kneeled. I stood there, staring at his body, taking brief glimpses of the thick curve in the front of his shorts. Sniffing the air for the slight aroma of his cologne, I inhaled deeply.

The intimacy between Nate and I had dwindled. He was often away on travel, and even when he was home, he was still working. I missed being caressed—and really, I missed being *fucked*—and in that moment, I wanted Vic. After manipulating the disposal with some s-shaped tool, Vic stood up and flipped on the disposal switch. It was working again. While he washed his hands in my sink, I thanked him graciously and proceeded to ask him intrusive questions to draw out his visit. I mentioned that I hadn't seen Carrie in a while and asked about her well-being. Vic said he and Carrie were separated. He had a gleam in his eye when he said it. Certain that he picked up on my surging pheromones, I coyly smirked back. I so deeply wanted to be seen again, to be touched like my body was a goddess's temple, to be admired, and to be tenderly handled.

We moved closer to one another. I thanked him again, and he softly grabbed my hand while accepting my gratitude. He squeezed my hand with a bit more pressure. I leaned into him. My heaving chest was against his; he gazed down into my eyes, cupped his arm around my lower spine, and drew me further in. I could feel his pulse. He bent down slightly until his lips met mine. He kissed me unapologetically and sucked on my tongue softly. Our bodies swayed back and forth against my kitchen counter. Reaching down between his legs, I could feel his bone-hard presence, thick and perfectly sized. I stroked him. He lifted my arms above my head and pulled my shirt off. His tongue moved from my lips to my neck, and then to my breast. I closed my eyes to absorb the moment.

We made our way to the floor, while never once lifting our hands from one another, partially naked on the cool tile. In that instance, I didn't think about Nate or the kids. I was fully entranced by the sexual desires and romantic feelings that had been devoid from my everyday life. With a formidable grip, he pulled my panties down from underneath my tennis skirt, slid them over my feet, and threw them behind his head and onto the floor. Vic spread my legs wide, like a frog leaping into a murky pond. He gripped my legs firmly, while gently biting my inner thighs, and made his way up to my wet jewels. Oh, was I wet! I hadn't felt my moistness pool and flow so abundantly in such a long time. He gently licked and fingered my womanly tender spots until I exploded. Then I welcomed him inside me, clasping tightly to his statuesque arms, like a bull rider trying to keep her grip. His powerful thrusts took me into overdrive. His pelvis rubbed against my clitoris with every stroke. He turned me to the side, one leg in the air, and continued to pound my kitty. I came again. Vic tilted forward, brushing against my breast, our lips lightly touching, and with his penis hard as stone, he took one last firm stroke, erupting his volcanic creamy magma into my starry pulsating capsule.

We lay quietly on the floor for a few moments, with me in his arms. No conversation was necessary. Shortly after, I walked Vic to the front door. There was a quiet exchange of goodbyes, never meant to be carried out again, and I closed the door, internally smiling.

Damn. I need to mop the floor.

One Word

One word is all I need
From the lips of my beloved
One word is all I need
That word shifts my thoughts
Inspires my world and
Takes hold of my inner being
It pushes me to the highest platforms of humanity
One word is all I need
That word elicits coital eruption
Calms my spirit
Exposes my inner lighthouse
Illuminating my beautiful soul
Thank you, my love,
For that
One word

Drowning in Work: Noa

This is my sixth work trip of the year, and it's only April. I'm one of the newest attorneys at the law firm, and we are always sent on travel assignments. It is possible that our status as single professionals helps with that decision, although the partners will never admit it. Most of them are older, and many have young families and spouses at home. Believe me, I understand, and if I had a family, I wouldn't want to travel this much, either. However, living out of a suitcase and in hotels what seems like every other week gets old, and truthfully, my date nights have consisted of me, myself, and I—along with all the legal documents and records pending my review. Just what every single woman dreams of!

I honestly can't remember the last time I had a date. Wait—I do remember. It was four months ago, with Cash Sounders, an attorney from another law firm, who was introduced to me by a mutual friend. Cash was a very good-looking man, and as you would suspect, he was tall, dark, and handsome. He was a 35-year-old successful attorney who made partner by the age of 32, drove a 1970 Black Chevy Chevelle, and lived in a downtown high-rise apartment. He was educated, successful, and had good taste. I looked at him and thought, *The Lord has answered my prayers.* We met at a quaint, high-end Italian restaurant called Mia Cucina.

Of course, I wore my signature black minidress with strappy gold heels; my legs were smooth and glistening—and let me not fail to mention that my makeup was flawless, and I smelled spectacular, since I was wearing Louis Vuitton Symphony perfume. I coifed my hair up in a loose bun, sexy yet sophisticated. I was ready for the night.

Cash walked up to me, looking dashing in his expensive slacks and crisp white shirt, simple but striking. We greeted each other and continued inside to be seated. We ordered wine and appetizers and proceeded with light conversation—rather, *he* proceeded with light conversation. He talked about himself all night: his courtroom wins, his jury-dazzling displays, his beloved presence at the firm, and even his college grades. All that Dean's list bullshit. He even showed me selfies of himself on his cell phone. Who *does* that? I do believe Cash was more impressed with himself than any mother could be of their own offspring. I sat there at the table, mustering a weak smile throughout the whole evening. Cash never once asked anything about me—not even if I enjoyed my meal. I was so ready for the date to be done. Finally, I just told him I needed to get home to my dog—yep, the one I don't have. After a quick side hug, I exited with my take-home box in hand, disappointed with the evening.

It's been seven months, and I haven't had another date since. Recently, I switched from battery-operated toys to rechargeable ones. What was I thinking? Nothing worse than prepping your mind for a brief satisfying moment—only for the damn thing to die during the best part of your fantasy or when you're about to climax. Nowadays, I make every attempt to charge them at least once a week, so they're always ready for my quick solo sexual play, but at least I get to fantasize—and I *do* allow my imagination to wander.

You see, how I imagined my night with Cash was *way* different than how it played out. Let me take you on my imaginary date with the oh-so-dashing Cash.

We greet each other just the same. He's still handsome as fuck, and I am just as sexy in my black dress, showing my long, slender, glistening legs and newly pedicured toes—and yes, smelling like perky, rose-covered titties—and my hot pussy is ready. His eyes speak to me, very much approving of my appearance and eliciting an almost palpable sexual passion. I tingle inside. My body is pleading for him to just take me, *now,* but of course, I'm a lady, so I walk next to him confidently, strutting all my strong, sexy, feminine energy.

We walk to our table, and Cash insists that the waiter let him seat me instead. Once seated, he gently squeezes my arms before making his way to his chair, as if he has no choice but to touch me. His hands are strong and manly. We order appetizers—bruschetta, calamari, lobster bites—and a bottle of champagne. He's quick-witted and smart. We laugh, and we are so engaged in our conversation that the waiter returns six times to inquire if and when we will be ready to order our meal.

Cash is smart and sexy, with a great sense of humor, and he's successful… oh, I am having his baby tonight on this very same table. I'm not sure if I really even want kids, but I'm willing to if this sexy, rich, good-teeth-having, fascinating man is going to be my baby daddy. Plus, Rachel from my office said that it has been confirmed: Cash has good dick. His Playboy behavior is well known.

We talk for what feels like several hours—although it has been only two. The sexual tension is as heavy as one of the leading cast members from "My 600lb Life." Cash invites me to his condo for after-dinner drinks. I acquiesce. I caught a Lyft here from my home, so we walk hand in hand to the parking garage where Cash's car is parked.

Our laughter fizzles to a mellow silence, and a subdued sensuality. We make our way to the passenger side of the car—and that's when Cash thrusts me against the door, and we begin to kiss passionately. He runs his hands across my breast and then pulls me closer to him, locking our tongues. After about five minutes of making out, we decide to make our way to our nearby destination.

Chivalrously, he opens the passenger door, so I can be seated, and then he cooly walks around to the driver's side. Cash settles into the driver's seat, cocks his head in my direction, and gives me an "I-want-to bang-your-pussy-*now*" kind of look. He grabs my knee, pulls me in close, and begins kissing me again— this time, even more intensely. Cash runs his hand between my legs, pulls my panties to the side, and begins circling his fingers around my clit, then he licks my juices from his fingers. I pull my panties down, and I can feel his eyes examining every move I make with lustrous hope. My body is hot with carnal potency and dewy in the right spot. I unbuckle his pants and pull them down to the floor of the car. I have to, I *need* to! His rock-hard dick, facing due north without a wobble, needs pleasure from me, and I *have* to stick that big handsome thing in my mouth.

I want to suck all of him, and I will. I bend my head down and commence running my tongue along the shaft of his penis. His eyes roll into the back of his head, and he moans softly.

Cash gently touches my chin, signaling for me to come back up. I straddle him with my long legs and pony up. It's a lock-and-key fit. My hips start moving up and down, swirling at a steady pace…

Buzz, Buzz, Buzz… Oh, shit, that's my phone. Really, right now? In the middle of my fantasy? Ugh.

"Hello," I answered.

"Hey Noa, are you up? This is Cash."

Shit.

My song for Cash is "I Want to Sex You Up" by Color Me Badd.

Say It Again

I rocked and swayed over the cresting of the waves
fitted tighter than fresh fish in a basket
Before yesterday, my skin glimmered like morning dew and
captured
the admiration of the highest chiefs
"You are lovely."
"Say it again."
"You are lovely."
A whirlwind fraught with devastation and despair
likened my skin to dirt and took not
notice or care of the jewel erected before them
They defaced it, they stomped it, they burned it
Stripped it of its precious minerals
but the ancestors said,
"You are lovely."
"Say it again."
"You are lovely."
You radiate like a field of spring flowers reflecting the sun's rays
Your majestic beauty cannot be hidden
They will envy you
They will attempt to move Heaven and Earth to dim
your fire

but your embers glow, too, and cannot be hidden
You dance when there should be tears
You levitate when you should have fallen
and again, the ancestors spoke:
"You are lovely."
"Say it again."
"You are lovely."

Lincoln

*"Yesterday's unchastities haunt the shadows of tomorrow and
billow to the surface like debris after a historic flood."*
—Vachon

It was a shock to all of Lincoln's friends when he told them
that his and Elena's relationship was growing more serious—
especially since he was a 32-year-old physical therapist, whom
they had never known to date a woman longer than three
months, give or take a few days. In fact, Lincoln was quite the
playboy, and his sexual soirees even made some of the other men
feel intimidated and often left them clutching their figurative
pearls. Lincoln had good looks, charm, a decent income, and no
kids—at least, none that he knew of.

That brisk October evening, at Lincoln's two-bedroom flat,
he and four of his good friends gathered for a much-anticipated
occasion to catch up over drinks, food, and a few games of pool.
Several months had passed since the crew had last met, because of
their busy careers and family responsibilities, and not to mention
that Drew, Griff, and Joel all had wives and children. Matt was
divorced but had one 4-year-old son with his ex-wife Marissa.

Lincoln was excited to have his friends join him at his
place. In his whitewashed brown brick walled galley kitchen,

he prepared his famous pulled pork nachos, guacamole, and lemon pepper wings. He also made certain to have a bottle of Greenwood Whiskey, Highway Vodka, and a couple of packs of Sankofa Beers, seated artfully on the counter, ready for the first pour.

The doorbell rang. Lincoln, in his black pullover zipper sweater and tan jeans, untied the apron from around his waist and greeted Matt and Griff at the door. With a boisterous greeting, Matt and Griff made their way to the kitchen and set their host's gifts on the counter, which comprised of a bottle of Uncle Nearest from Matt and Griff's homemade chocolate poundcake. Drew and Joel arrived shortly after. Drew, as usual, showed up with nothing more than excuses as to why he didn't bring anything, and Joel brought the cigars.

On the back side of the pool table, Lincoln opened the double glass doors leading out to his patio; to allow in fresh air and so they could smoke their cigars outdoors while remaining part of the conversation at the pool table.

"So," said Griff. "You're really thinking about settling down with this chick?"

"Yeah," nodded Lincoln, with a slight smirk on his face while balancing one hand on the pool table and with the pool stick in the other.

"What is it about Elena that's *so* different than all the other chicks you have dated?" inquired Drew. He was seated in a bar stool behind the pool table and embracing a plateful of nachos. "Man, I'm curious, because *we* know what kind of ferocious sexual appetite you have."

Before Lincoln could respond, Matt interjected from the lounge chair on the patio, "Ahh, remember in 2006 when Drew came home from basic training?"

"Oh, shit! That's right!" exclaimed Drew. "Linc, picked us up in that big ass Navigator with the blow-up mattress in the trunk and took us to that hole-in-the-wall club down on sixth and Jefferson. That shit was wild. What single dude drives a big ass Navigator and why the hell did you need a blow-up mattress in the back?"

Joel, casually leaning on the frame of the opened exterior glass door, smoking one of his cigars, expounded on the conversation. "Drew, you're right that shit was wild. I was so drunk. And who the fuck were those girls? I just remember dancing, doing shots and next thing you know, we were at Linc's cheap-ass apartment with like three women. His only furniture was a couch and a bed," Joel giggled.

Lincoln, in his cocky stance, bent low and took the next shot on the pool table. He rubbed his hand over his mouth, and made a soft chuckle, but refrained from responding.

"I couldn't partake in none of that shit. Marissa and I were engaged at the time, and I saw that shit going south real quick," noted Matt.

Lincoln was still quiet.

"I mean, it was sexy as fuck, watching three women kiss and play with each other. Sexy, but ... to be honest, that was one of my fantasies, but I quickly realized that it was only meant to be a fantasy. I couldn't really do that shit in real life," said Joel. "It was too much for me. I will stick to one chick at a time."

"I was too scared to get into some shit," replied Drew. I had just got back from basic and Linc, you were passing around Viagra like it was Tylenol. Hell no."

"Hey, my boy Griff here had himself a good time," laughed Lincoln, while patting Griff on his back at the pool table.

"What?" asked Matt. "Me, Drew and Joel caught a taxi home."

"Look, that one in the black tights was hot," noted Griff. So, yeah, we got busy, she and I, but I chickened out after that. I couldn't keep going and sleep with the other women, too. Next thing I knew, the women were kissing and performing oral sex on each other, and Lincoln was blowing through all the pussy. He was screwing one, while she was doing the other chick, and this shit went on for hours. I watched for a bit and took my ass to bed on that hard-ass sofa. Every time I rolled over, I could still hear them going at it. When I woke up later that morning, Lincoln was asleep, with all three ladies in his bed."

"And didn't you sleep with Chris Denton's mom when we were in college?" Matt asked Lincoln as he was making his way inside.

"Ugh, I was at least 20, and she was always coming up to campus, bringing food with those short-ass dresses on. What do you expect? Momma was fine, and she wasn't *my* momma," explained Lincoln, "but look, fellas, I think it's time for me to settle down and have a little me running around here. My first sexual encounter was at 15, and she was 16… church basement. I've been fucking for a long time, and I have had all the pussy I could ever want, and Elena is just perfect for me. She's a schoolteacher. She's kind, smart… beautiful, everything that all those other women weren't, and it's just something about her. So, yeah." The other men looked on… astounded and pleased that the playboy was soon to be settled down.

Ten years later, Lincoln and Elena were living the typical family life. Lincoln now owned his own physical therapy business called Stronger PT, and Elena worked as a schoolteacher at the school where their two children—Daniel 5, and Liza, 7—attended. For Lincoln, life was good, and Elena was everything he knew she would be, but after 10 years of marriage, Lincoln found himself acquiring a lustful eye again. The last thing he wanted was to hurt Elena and destroy their family, so he consciously thwarted his desire to flirt with intention.

One cold winter afternoon, Lincoln had the day off and headed to a local coffee shop within walking distance of their home. While walking out of Bit's Coffee and Brew, Lincoln decided to venture next door into the *Bye Books* bookstore. He had often thought about visiting but never had the chance to. The bell above the door loudly clanged as he opened the glass compartmented wood door. Lincoln, with his hands in his thick grey trench coat, shivered a bit, as if to shake off the brittle cold. A small, pale faced, old woman with long stringy gray hair, tied back with a plaid scarf, wearing a long multi-colored skirt, walked in from behind a beaded curtain.

"May I help you find something, dear?" she asked while looking Lincoln squarely in the face.

"No, ma'am. I just wanted to check out your store. I've never been in here before," stated Lincoln.

"Oh, but *you've* been here before," giggled the older woman. "My name is Tess."

"I'm sorry. What do you mean by that? I've been here before?" asked Lincoln, perplexed.

"Well, my dear. I read you when you walked through the door. You love your wife, but you have desires. It's who you are. You've been here before multiple times, and you've always lusted after women and have had many wonderful erotic encounters in your lifetimes."

"Look, many men… most men have desires, and I'm sure you knew that before I walked in here. I don't know what you're trying to do, and I assure you that I've never been here before. Maybe I should leave," said Lincoln nervously.

"Wait! Take this crystal." Tess turned and reached for a green crystal from a shelf behind the counter. She turned back to Lincoln. "I know it doesn't look like anything special, but when the desires become overpowering, go to a quiet place, alone, and rub this crystal five times counterclockwise. Let crystal show you who you once were, and remember to set a timer. Start with two minutes, but no longer than eight," said Tess softly and slowly.

Lincoln cautiously opened his hand, while Tess gently placed the crystal in his palm and closed his fist around it. He placed it in his pocket. Confused about the visit, Lincoln circled back towards the exit, haphazardly walking into a bookshelf before leaving and making his way back home. The bell above the door loudly announced his departure.

Throughout much of the evening, Lincoln thought about the crystal now planted on the desk in his home library. Elena observed Lincoln's internal preoccupation at their kitchen table during supper. She ordered Daniel and Liza to get ready for bed. Once they departed, she turned to Lincoln, who sat to the left of her. "Everything all right? You seem distracted. You've barely touched your dinner," Elena said.

"Ah, no. I'm sorry. I'm fine. Uh, I went into the little bookstore next to the coffee shop this morning after I got my coffee. I wanted to check it out. Have you been in there?"

"I can't say that I have, but it seems like it's had an impact on you, so maybe I should," said Elena sarcastically. "Okay, so what happened in there?"

"No, nothing. It's just that the woman in the shop there was strange," said Lincoln with a faraway gaze.

"Should I be worried about this *woman*? Is she turning you on?" curiously asked Elena.

"God, no! She's an old hag, literally. She just reminds me of an old hippie witch with potions and shit."

"I'm not following. What's it to you?" asked Elena.

"Just the vibe. That's all. It was weird," said Lincoln while combing over his food with his fork. "I've never felt such strangeness, that's all. It was different."

"Okay…" replied Elena, with a perplexed look on her face, but she restrained herself from asking more questions about a situation that she didn't feel deserved much more attention. Elena gathered their plates from the table and softly kissed Lincoln on the forehead as she made her way to the kitchen sink.

Later that evening, after Elena and the kids went to bed, Lincoln found himself wrapped in his deep navy-blue cashmere robe, an investment he proudly made several years back, seated at his desk, sipping whiskey from his favorite glass, and staring at this "magical" crystal. *It's not possible*, he thought, *but, what if, in some weird way, the hippie witch is right? What if I do as she says, and I rub it like she told me to, and nothing happens? Then no harm done, and she was just fucking with me.*

"You're just fucking with me, old lady. I know this is bullshit. I'm going to just play along, so I can be done with it," said Lincoln out loud.

Lincoln reached for the crystal, picked it up, and stared at it with uncertainty for several seconds. He removed his cell phone from his pocket, placed it face-up, and set the timer for two minutes and 30 seconds. It was 10:17. He started the timer.

He placed his index finger at the base of the crystal and began rubbing it counterclockwise slowly. He counted each time he completed a full turn. "One." There was a brief spark. "Two." Another spark. *How can this be*? "Three." Another spark. This time, the glow lasted longer. "Four." The crystal glowed even longer. "Five."

Lincoln found himself standing in an alleyway, in between whitewashed stone buildings, gazing down at the cobbled brick road underneath his lightly tanned feet. He was cladded in a red kilt heavy skirt, a silver armored breast plate, brown strapped sandals, and with a heavy sword affixed to his left hip. As he stood there, Lincoln centered in on the sounds of the world he was now in. Sounds such as the horse hooves that thumped heavily against the stone road, the rumble of large-wheeled carts being pulled through streets; street vendors calling for people to buy their bread and tapestries and mules screeching. The smell too was memorable, a mix of spices, perfumes, livestock, and freshly baked bread.

As he made his way out of the alley, Lincoln noticed a young muscular built, dark curly-haired soldier waving wildly at him and coming towards him, weaving his way through the crowd.

"Cato! Cato! Cato, my friend. We've been looking for you for days. We thought one of the Gaulish soldiers had captured you, but you seem to have all your limbs and are as healthy as a horse. Good to see you're back. Rather, should I call you by your official title, Primus Pilus Cato Maximus, Chief Centurium? You were magnificent in battle, sir. Such an honor to be in battle with you, but where have you been if I may ask?" asked Flavian, one of Cato's fellow soldiers.

"Flavian, it's good to see you, too. I'm sorry for my brief disappearance. I had to ensure that no further trouble from the Gauls would arise," said Cato. Lincoln was astounded that with full certainty, he responded to Flavian and recognized this other past world, while being conscious of his world at home with Elena and the kids. It was like puppeteering his own dream world that illogically felt tangible and familiar.

"Would you like me to let the Praefectus Castrorum know of your return? Oh, and since it's been a few days, a certain lady—or rather, *ladies*—have been asking for you down at the brothel." Flavian smirked.

"Indeed. Announce my return from the battlefield, and I will show myself first thing tomorrow morning and deliver the news about the war. First, I need not let the ladies wait, and I could use a beer or two," smiled Cato.

As dusk was approaching, Lincoln, cloaked as Cato, wound his way through a series of narrow streets and back alleys, passing by women and children seated on the stoops with soot smeared faces, begging for any amount of denarius to procure even the smallest loaf of bread. The dark evening streets of Rome were often plagued with impoverished tenants and violent criminals, but all of whom knew not to come against anyone in the Roman Army. Broken large pottery vases lay strewn against the walls of the buildings. Some were previously filled with wines and beer and others with food and oils. As he neared the brothel, there were several young men and women, scantily dressed, standing around the dirty walls of shabby buildings, and some walking purposelessly around. Cato could sense the stares and hear the chatter acknowledging his presence elicited by his military uniform. He knocked on the heavy wooden door with intention. An older woman, wearing a thin white veiled dress adorned with sequence, greeted Cato at the door. She appeared surprised and pleased all the same.

"Good evening, Centurium Maximus. Your presence here at the lupanar has been missed." The matron swung open her arm, ushering Cato in.

The lupanar was dark and cavernous, with a labyrinth of paths leading to a multitude of rooms. One room operated as a backdoor tavern, another as a small for-profit kitchen offering soups, stews, local bread, and fruits, while many others were small rooms where more intimate sexual improprieties occurred. Some of the fornication conspicuously took place directly in the halls, atop a barrage of pillows, blankets, and other soft bedding. For the more prestigious patrons, there were a few bath houses towards the back end of the lupanar, which were typically where Cato frequented.

Not long after Cato entered the establishment, a maiden offered him a beer. They were well acquainted with his beverage preferences—not wine, like most, but rather, a generous-sized mug filled with beer. With sheer satisfaction, Cato stood against the cool stone wall, guzzled his beer, and simultaneously watched the erotic spectacles that adorned the halls. In front of him was a middle-aged man, seated naked with his legs spread wide on the makeshift bed, while a female worker, rested on her knees, pleasured him with her mouth. The man pulled her hair like a jockey holding the reins. Next to them were three males, sexually engaged with one another. In a separate corner were two naked female workers taking pleasure in one another. The woman on top held up the leg of the other woman, scissoring her, deeply rubbing her loins back and forth against the other woman, moaning in sheer pleasure. Cato enthusiastically watched, and Lincoln's guilty erotic desires were increasingly fulfilled.

A young male worker adorned with thick eyeliner, wearing only a sheer shoulder scarf, identified as a worker by his white rope bracelet, demurely approached Cato, implicitly offering his services. Cato shook his head, declining the young man's services, as he had never had even the slightest attraction to men. No, Cato patiently waited for Ophelia. She was his favorite, and she often brought along her choice of women to help service him. Ophelia was a big-breasted, curvy woman of average height, with long, dark, wavy hair and deep green eyes. She had learned Cato's sexual needs, how his body responded to her moves, her style of play, and even her scent. She knew when to tease and when to go hard. Occasionally, she even took care of him in other ways, like ensuring that he had a good meal, preparing baths for him, and running minor errands. Because of this, Cato had developed more than just sensual feelings for Ophelia; he deeply cared for her and expressed his affection by paying her extra denarii—or even paying for her housing costs occasionally—but he also knew that she could never be more than a prostitute to him.

She walked in through the dark halls with a slow, sexy strut, donning a colorful floor length dress, but sheer enough for one to visualize her thick hips and dark nipples. Ophelia fixed her gaze on Cato and advanced towards him with an almost devious intention. She seductively grabbed his hand and pulled in close to him and whispered in his ear, "you were missed. Come."

Ophelia held Cato's hand tightly and led him down the corridor to his favorite bath house, walking past vats full of wines and simple oils. As they walked through the dark hall, Lincoln spotted a woman standing stoutly and intently eyeing them. She looked like a younger version of Tess. Their eyes met, but no words were exchanged.

The bath house had a large stone tub nestled in the room's corner, and featured colorful blankets, an assortment of large pillows, a small table adorned with bottles of wine, two oil lamps, small vials of perfumed oils and there laid a small vat of olive oil on the floor. One maiden poured Cato a large glass of red wine, while the other helped to undress him, carefully removing his armored gear. Cato paid close attention to the placement of his items, particularly his sword. Ophelia's two helpers began titillating play with one another. It was part of the show. The two maidens kissed and fondled each other, and would often turn their eyes to Cato, making certain he was watching. Ophelia, on the other hand, undressed herself, retrieved a cup of oil and strolled over to Cato, who had situated himself on a large array of pillows, sipping his wine, happily viewing the show. Ophelia sat on her knees behind Cato and drizzled the warm oil over his shoulders until it ran down his back and down the front of his torso. She massaged his body with slow, firm strokes, beginning at the nape of his neck. While rubbing her oil slicked hands rigidly up and down his arms, and her large breast caressing his back, Ophelia whispered to Cato, "you like what you see?"

Cato, with a gentle nod, replied, "Yes."

The maidens' performance was an erotic display that Cato was taking immense pleasure in, and Lincoln felt like the little brother that had snuck in through the back door that no one knew was there. Both women were small in stature, with pocket-sized perky breast, nothing like Ophelia's voluptuousness. Junia, one of the maidens, wrapped round to the backside of Helvia, the other maiden. Both women were on their knees. Then Junia took her soft shawl and placed it between both of their legs and pulled the shawl back and forth, caressing their moist parts, and passionately kissed Helvia's back and neck. Junia then tied part of the wrap around her waist, keeping the rest of the sheer wrap stretched between their legs, to allow her to free up her left hand. She swayed her torso with rigor and clutched the wrap tight, putting pressure on their swollen lady part. Junia, in her dominate role, placed a wooden tool in the shape of a penis into the knot tied around her waist. She slid her hand down on Helvia's back and pushed her head towards the floor, raised Helvia's right leg and inserted the wooden dildo into her wet orifice and thrusted her repeatedly with vigor.

Ophelia reached her hands around Cato's waist, gripped his hard wood, squeezed, and pulled back and forth until Cato breathed heavily, his gaze focused on the maidens. When Cato appeared less fixated on the maidens and fully aroused from the stroking of his penis, Ophelia pivoted herself to face him, straddled his waist, and slowly circled her dripping wet cavity onto his hard wood. She rose up and lowered herself down, circling her hips and controlling her vaginal grip as she rested down firmly each time. For Cato, Ophelia's vaginal grips were stronger than most maidens' hand jobs. Ophelia circled, gripped, and pounded repeatedly.

Lincoln heard a distant beeping. *Oh, shit,* he thought. *My time is up.*

Ophelia rested firmly down one last time.

"Oh!" Lincoln cried out in ecstasy as he awakened from his dream world, with the timer beeping rapidly. Lincoln had come all over his blue cashmere robe. Beads of sweat clung to his forehead.

He glanced down at his beeping phone. It was 10:19 PM. *How the fuck is that possible?* thought Lincoln. He had spent several hours in the dream world, but only two minutes in the real world. He also wondered how it felt so real. Part of Lincoln feared that it was not just a dream world. He could smell Ophelia's fragrance. It was on his skin.

Lincoln sat at his desk for several moments, analyzing what had just occurred. Maybe he didn't smell Ophelia's fragrance, rather, maybe it was an overactive neural dream experience. He couldn't comprehend it. Lincoln resigned his thoughts for the night, showered, and went to bed, feeling confused, giddy, and satisfied.

Over the next few days, the crystal remained conspicuously placed in the middle of Lincoln's large, clean, ornate desk, untouched. The experience provided Lincoln with a level of sexual satisfaction that he hadn't felt in years. It was not that sex with Elena was unenjoyable, but he had an insatiable craving for explicit sexual encounters that he knew Elena would never partake in. Although he was temporarily satisfied, Lincoln remained curious and confused. He decided to pay Tess a visit and went to the bookstore.

The bell once again alerted Lincoln's entrance into *Bye Books.* Lincoln, dressed in black scrubs and a blue parka jacket, keenly scanned the room, looking for any clues to this confusing puzzle. He was so focused on procuring any overlooked details, he narrowly missed Tess standing adjacently in the back corner of the room. Lincoln slightly jumped at her presence.

Tess, still dressed like a hippie witch, donning a headscarf, a colorful blouse, and a sweeping, floor-length skirt, flatly greeted Lincoln. "You're back. I'm guessing you've used the crystal, and now you have questions."

"What kind of fantasy crystal is this, and why is the dream *so* vivid? I mean, I still had her scent on me. Shit—at least, my mind believed I did," whispered Lincoln, as he scanned the room anyone who might be listening.

"My dear, this is your life, not a dream. Rather, it's oh so very real. And it's a reminder. It's who you were and who you are. It's your opportunity to get it right. Though you must be careful. Don't extend your time past eight minutes and don't visit too often. You could be playing with fire," murmured Tess.

Lincoln sighed, nodded to Tess, and turned to leave the store. Then he remembered he wanted to question Tess about her appearance at the lupanar in his dream world, but when he turned back around, Tess had already retreated behind the beaded curtain.

Sexual desires emerged in Lincoln again. His experience with crystal was powerful and satisfying, and now he had the courage to try it again. As he'd done previously, Lincoln waited for Elena and the kids to retreat to bed before going to his office.

Anticipating uninhibited sexual pleasure, he pulled his cellphone from the pocket of his robe, placed it on the desk, and set the timer—this time for three minutes. He quickly picked up the crystal and tapped "start" on his phone. Lincoln rubbed the crystal counterclockwise. One… two… three… four… five.

He found himself in a small African village where he was a revered Zulu warrior with three wives. Lincoln's sexual experience with his wives—coupled with his powerful role— gave him great pleasure. Many of the tribe's women and their fathers—who wished for their daughters to be married into Zulu military royalty under King Shaka—sought after the esteemed Zulu warrior. Upon waking from his trance-like state, Lincoln found a small white bead lying in the crutch of his palm.

Over the next few days, Lincoln repeated his late-night departures to his office, escaping to his former lives, from Zula warrior to Zen Dynasty leader and finally to an Egyptian prince. He experienced his profound greatness in his past lives and bore witness to his intense sexual appetite, and with each trip, Lincoln brought back a token: a sword from China, and a papyrus note from Egypt. He hid his tokens in an old wicker chest, hidden in the corner of the closet in his home office.

Lincoln achieved a greater level of confidence in his use of the crystal. He had set the timer for no longer than three minutes and 30 seconds on his previous visits, but now, on his fifth attempt, he felt comfortable enough to set the timer for six minutes. He put his finger on the crystal.

Counterclockwise-One…Two…Three…Four…Five.

By way of the enigmatic crystal, Lincoln again embarked upon a journey within his Roman persona, Cato. He was back. Lincoln could not manipulate or influence the setting of his adventures. Nonetheless, he was ecstatic about being in Cato's internal presence again.

The Roman Empire's leadership was in pronounced turbulence. Cato, in his newly appointed role, sat amongst the Roman Emperor and the Senators, keenly listening to the spirited debate. As a new young senator, Cato developed an arrogance about him. He felt he could have any woman in Rome. Cato was important and much desired. He visited the lupanar more often, engaging in wild erotic plays that left him so fatigued that he often just stayed the night, and Ophelia was always his main event.

The Senate's chaos extended into the late evening, and Cato, growing bored and tired, was anxiously waiting to make his way to the lupanar. When they realized they would not reach an agreement before the end of the night, the Senate decided to pause.

Cato sprang from his Senate post and bolted out of the building, relieved. As he was making his way to the brothel, Cato spotted a young woman packing up linens and goods from her store in the street market. She was the most beautiful woman he had ever seen. It was dark, but the moon shone brightly on her glowing skin, and Cato noticed every part of her beauty: her wavy black hair, her startling, glassy blue eyes, and her soft, sweet face. She was magnificent. The young woman caught Cato peering at her, looked up from packing her cart, and smiled at him sweetly.

"Excuse me. Excuse me, dear lady. Let me assist you with that. It is dark out here and no woman as beautiful as you should be out after dark alone." Cato eagerly skipped to greet the woman at her cart.

"There were patrons who arrived late to purchase linens they needed for a large wedding. They had many decisions to make. You're wearing a toga. Are you part of the Senate?" asked the young matron.

"Why, yes, I am. Cato. My name is Cato. With whom am I in the wonderful presence of?"

"Flora," she said. I'm one of the merchants here. I make and sell these lovely linens."

"Pleasure to meet you. Allow me to help you home."

"Thank you. I would like that."

Cato walked Flora to her home a short distance from the market, striking up light conversation on the way. Cato was smitten by Flora's sweet demeanor, and the way she laughed at his silly stories. He instantly knew that he never wanted to part from her. After helping Flora unpack her cart, Cato finally made his way to the lupanar—though Flora occupied his mind. Once he arrived, Cato received a royal welcome, with a celebrity-like reception. Ophelia quickly greeted him with a light kiss and handed him a mug of beer. She felt as though she were obliquely *his* woman, as Cato pursued no one to the extent that he pursued her. He made her feel desired and worthy. Ophelia assumed that the only reason Cato had not married her was because of social norms. She knew he could never marry a prostitute. Ophelia ushered him to his favorite bath house and offered him a large bowl of hot soup, and a considerable piece of crusty bread. Cato welcomed the late meal since the Senate meeting had run well past dinnertime.

The meal was hearty, flavorful, and satisfying. He thanked Ophelia for the provisions, and then lay back on the pillows, tucking his hands behind his head, fully clothed, with Flora occupying his thoughts.

Ophelia scrutinized the change in his behavior. "Is everything all right?" she asked. "It appears your thoughts are somewhere else. Would you care to talk? I don't know much about what happens in those Senate assemblies, but I am certain that I can be of some assistance—even if I'm nothing more than a good ear."

"No, it's not that. It's nothing, really." Cato lay there quietly, deep in his own thoughts.

"Well, let me at least ease your tension. You just lay there and let me do all the work." Ophelia gathered Cato's garment around his waist and began to run her tongue down the shaft of his hard flute. She pleasured him until he erupted in her mouth. Though satisfied, thoughts of Flora still danced in his head. He kissed Ophelia on the forehead and rested next to her momentarily. It had been customary for Cato to stay the night with Ophelia at the brothel, but tonight, Cato shortened his stay, as he wished to meet Flora in the early morning on her way to set up at the local market. For the first time since their coupling, Ophelia felt distance and uncertainty in her and Cato's relationship.

As Cato made his way through the dark, narrow streets, there was a light shining through one lone window in an apartment above. He glanced up and there a woman appeared, glaring directly at him. Tess.

Flora's presence disrupted his brief slumber. Cato tossed and turned for the next few hours in his bed. He immediately adored and loved this woman whom he did not even know. Something about her amazed him. Cato knew that Flora was meant to be his wife. That morning, Cato awakened early, dressed in clean layman's clothing, doused himself with his finest oil, and rushed out to meet Flora at her apartment.

In reality, Lincoln was riding shotgun. He was conscious of the experience but had no control of the navigation. As time passed, Lincoln could feel himself merging with Cato. Yet, he still thought of these two worlds as separate. Unreal, but real.

"It's early. Good morning. To what do I owe the pleasure?" smiled Flora.

My goodness, she is beautiful.

"I just thought you could use the help this morning. Make your life a little simpler."

"I would like that," stated Flora.

Cato walked her to her spot at the market, joyfully conversing with her and gleefully soaking in her existence. Flora found Cato to be a gentleman. He was funny, kind, and generous. Over the next few weeks, Cato split his time between the Senate and Flora. He endowed no time at the lupanar or with Ophelia. Rather, Cato used this time to cultivate his relationship with Flora, and he dreamt of a time where he could he feel her loins solely as his wife.

Beep, beep, beep, beep. Lincoln breathed deeply and looked down at the timer.

Five minutes. It's only been five minutes, but I spent weeks in Rome with Flora.

Lincoln sat there at his desk for several more minutes, analyzing his visit and his feelings. He couldn't stop now. Lincoln was fully invested in his Roman life, and he too felt something for Flora, real or unreal. He also felt remorse about Cato's unannounced distance from Ophelia. He could only imagine what she was feeling. Lincoln turned off the lights in the office, and joined Elena in bed, almost feeling like a stranger.

"You want to tell me what's going on with you?" Elena asked Lincoln first thing in the morning, while they were still lying in bed. "You don't come to bed with me most nights, and we haven't had sex like we normally do. What's going on, Lincoln? Is it porn? Are you watching porn? Are you cheating? You're running around here acting strange… all in your own head. I don't understand. Matt and Joel both said they've been trying to call you, and you haven't answered them. What the hell, Lincoln?"

"No! It's not that. It's not any of those things. I've just been stressed out about work and the business. I've lost Tim. He was one of my best therapists, and now I'm going to have to fill in more. You're right; I've been in my own head lately, and I'm sorry." Lincoln couldn't bring himself to tell Elena the truth about the crystal; then again, he wasn't certain that she would believe him. In sincerity, Lincoln wanted to keep it hidden, and for it to be his secret refuge.

Elena reluctantly conceded, disbelieving Lincoln's story, but she would leave the matter alone for now.

Over the next couple of months, Lincoln used the crystal near-daily, staying up to nine minutes at a time. He now varied the times when he used it, so Elena would feel that he was still present in their family life. Instead of nightly, Lincoln sometimes used the crystal early in the morning, before Elena and the kids awakened, and other times, he used it midday, visiting his Roman life as Cato and embarking on a new life with Flora. Lincoln never returned to any of his previous destinations.

Why? Why does the crystal only take me back to Rome? What's the significance?

Lincoln continued to acquire tokens from each of his visits to Rome. Some of his tokens included a pillow, Flora's hairbrush, Cato's strapped sandals, and a spoon, just to name a few. He hid them, along with the rest, in his office closet. Lincoln remained confused about how such items could make their way into this world, but the most peculiar occurrence was the change in Lincoln's hair. His hair texture had changed somewhat. Lincoln now sported soft, dark, loosely curled hair, which closely resembled Cato's. Elena joked, "I didn't know they were bringing back perms. Did your barber encourage you to do that to your hair? You should get your money back!"

He had spent nearly a year in Rome, and Cato was sure to ask Flora for her hand in marriage. Lincoln thought, *After marrying Flora, I'm done with the crystal. The old witch can have it back.*

He set the timer. 10 minutes and 30 seconds.

Counterclockwise…One…Two…Three…Four…Glowing…Five.

As Cato walked out of the Senate assembly, Tess walked intently towards him, meeting him at the lowest step of the Curia Julia. She grabbed his arm with a brute squeeze and gazed sharply into his eyes. "You, my dear, are pushing the boundaries. Cato, you must know that Lincoln lives within you, but Lincoln cannot stay!"

Lincoln knew that Tess was talking directly to *him*, not Cato, but somehow, Lincoln could sense that Cato was becoming conscious of Lincoln's spirit. Cato stared mutely back at Tess, with a flurry of thoughts floating around his head. To some extent, Cato understood what Tess was communicating, but all the same, he felt powerless. Tess released her grip on Cato's arm, gave him a furious look, and then walked away.

Days later, Cato met with Flora's family, to seek permission for her hand in marriage. August, Flora's father, was eager to accept Cato's request, as he knew Flora marrying into nobility would be valuable for the entire family. That night, like most of Cato's evenings, he met with Flora after her long workday in the market, helped load her items onto the cart and walked her home. Flora prepared a small dinner for them. The dinner was sufficient and tasty, and as they have become accustomed to, full of laughter and joy. Cato excused himself from the table and returned with a bouquet of flowers hidden behind his back. He walked up to Flora, who had remained seated at the table.

"Flora. This past year with you has been incredible. From the moment I saw you standing there in the moonlight, I realized you were my wife-in-waiting. You are as breathtaking as the morning dew. You are the envy of most women, and the insecurity of many a man. I wish only for you to be the bearer of my first-born son. I ask with great humbleness: Will you take my hand in marriage?"

"My father would have to agree," said Flora.

"He has already granted me his permission."

"Then so it shall be. Yes."

Cato was enamored about his upcoming wedding to Flora. He occasionally thought of Ophelia. He felt sad for her, and guilt often spilled from his heart, but his overwhelming love for Flora overshadowed his lust for Ophelia. There was uncertainty and upheaval in the Senate regarding the vacant Roman consul seat that could propel Rome into utter chaos, and because of this, the families of the upcoming bride and groom opted to have the wedding sooner, rather than later. Within weeks, Cato and Flora were married. Cato moved them into a large home in an affluential district of Rome, with servants to attend to the duties that most common wives would do. Flora would be busy with her new duties as a noble wife.

Flora and Cato consummated their marriage on their wedding night. It had been almost a year since he had pleasured a woman or received pleasure from a woman. He had poured his energy into his relationship with Flora, preparing to take her as his wife. He did not want any distractions, and Ophelia was an *enormous* distraction. Flora was a virgin, but over the last few months, she could feel her loins begin to tingle when Cato kissed her, and she became moist from his breath on her neck alone. So, that wedding night, Flora was ready to receive her husband. Cato had forgotten what it was like to sleep with a virgin. It was moist, warm, and tight. He went slow, not wanting to hurt her but also wanting to enjoy his new bride. After Flora's initial groans of pain, Cato eventually felt her relax, and her painful groans turned into passionate breathing. Flora had never imagined her body erupting in such pleasure.

One day, Flora said, "Husband, I have not had my monthlies since before our wedding. It's been three months, so it is assumed I am with child."

"Well, let Bacchus, God of Fertility, bless us with our first son," replied Cato with pride.

It had been over a year since Cato was in the company of Ophelia, and he felt like he owed her an explanation—especially now that he and Flora were with child. One afternoon, Cato retired early from his Senate duties and elected to pay Ophelia a visit at the lupanar. Although he and Flora were now married, it was customary for married men to seek pleasure at brothels. Therefore, it would not be sinful for Cato to be seen there. Cato followed the stone road with carved markings that directed patrons along their journey to the local lupanars. Stares and a brief silence greeted him upon entering. Ophelia observed the silence and measuredly turned around to see what was happening behind her. *Cato.* An amalgam of emotions inundated her very being. She was relieved to see him but also felt anger and hurt. Ophelia quickly made her way to him.

"I'm surprised to see you, but I welcome the visit," said Ophelia in a confident voice, trying to hide the pain.

"I'm sorry I've been away," replied Cato.

"I know. You got married. All of Rome has been chattering about it. I'm truly happy for you."

"If we may, can we retreat to the bathhouse to speak?"

Ophelia led Cato back to their usual bath house. Cato explained his disappearance and his love for Flora. He also acknowledged his feelings for Ophelia and his appreciation for her over the last few years. Ophelia missed him. She understood that Cato's time now belonged to Flora, but she wanted him to share, and she was willing to do whatever was necessary to pull Cato back into her life.

"I've missed you so," whispered Ophelia to Cato. "Let me please you like I've done time and time again."

Ophelia reached up and kissed Cato, and he returned the kiss. Cato missed her, too. He missed the way she made love to him. He missed how her body felt. Cato turned Ophelia away from him, bent her over until Ophelia's hands touched the ground, and she was nearly in a handstand, and he drummed her soft yoni until she throbbed on his penis, causing him to lose control. Cato released his essence into Ophelia. Pleasured.

Flora and Cato lived a peaceful, happy life, but pregnancy was uncomfortable for Flora—especially during sex. Over the next few weeks, Cato spent at least four days a week at the lupanar with Ophelia, delving into unsubdued ecstasy. Flora felt alone in Cato's recurrent abandonment, yet she was aware of her inability to quench his sexual demands. Ophelia, on the other hand, ensured that Cato's sexual desires were met. She listened keenly to his wishes and brought them all to life.

One evening, Cato wanted to spend the evening alone with Ophelia, with no other workers in the room. He wanted her in every way. Ophelia prepared a hot bath. She made certain to have a small vat of beer in the room, along with a few small snacks. Cato indulged in the beer, while watching Ophelia and admiring her curves and beauty. She was sexy. Naked, Ophelia took Cato by the hand and had him join her in the hot bath. She rubbed oils over his body, and he did the same to her. Cato spread Ophelia's legs and lay between them, kissing her passionately. He gently stroked her clitoris, and Ophelia leaned her head back, attentive to the nucleus of feelings between her thighs. Cato entered her. He wanted to take his time. He knew that once the baby was born, his time at the brothel would be even more restricted. The warm water ebbed and flowed with the movement of their bodies. Cato moved his neck back in a display of intense passion—only to see Flora standing right in front of him, with a look of disbelief, hurt, and anger.

Cato fretfully jumped out of the water. Ophelia reached back and grabbed his hand. Flora looked down at Ophelia in an angry stance and tried to push past Cato to get to her. Cato grabbed Flora's arm.

Beep… beep… beep. The timer. Ten minutes and 30 seconds gone.

Upon awakening from his trance, Lincoln looked up, only to find a dripping wet Ophelia, and an angry pregnant Flora staring at him with fear in their faces.

"Where are we?" asked Flora.

"What kind of dark magician are you?" inquired Ophelia.

Lincoln was stiff with horror. He had to get them back to their world. Lincoln grabbed the crystal, set the timer for only 30 seconds, and grabbed both of their hands. Cato was in the bath house again, but neither Ophelia nor Flora were there. For two hours, he scoured the city, looking for them to no avail.

Beep… beep… beep. 30 seconds gone.

The women were still there, in his office, motionless. Sweat trickled down the side of Lincoln's face. His pursed lips labored to push out his breaths. He glanced at the rock with disdain. He thought, "why in hell did I take that rock?" My life with Elena was complete. Stupid! Stupid! Stupid! Tess…"

The door opened. It was Elena. She peered at the women; one obviously with child and dressed like she was just in a local playwright and the other naked and dripping wet. "Lincoln! What the fuck is going on in here?"

Strong

I often profess that I came out of the womb this way
With a muscular attitude, a fierce stride,
and a jagged tongue
My back made of steel, and my skin of leather
Strong

My legs, like redwood trees, mighty, sturdy, with branches
meant to carry the burden of it all
Yet harsh seasons weaken my trunk,
break my branches, and sever my tongue
The burdens still come
They wobble and crawl until they make their way to me
Strong

There, like the lone seed blooming amid the summer heat
Against all odds of realization
I reemerge, ready to display my bright, colorful leaves,
giving aesthetic joy, and the humble usefulness of my nectar
Strong

But they take my nectar
They do not offer me water
I begin to wilt
Then rainfall invigorates my being at just the right moment

Nourishes my roots
Bones that have been broken grow stronger
Bracing for the oncoming weight to be inevitably
thrust upon them
Strong

My canopy grows far and wide
And becomes a haven to the feeble,
and a shelter to the unhoused
But they break my branches, damage my roots,
steal my nutrients *and* my seeds
Sap running down my trunk
And there are no offerings of a handkerchief
Recovery is not as quick anymore
Some of the bark, now permanently gone
Scars forever embedded
Bones possessing calcified fissures
Yet, I arise from the fight, renewed
Strong

My strength hasn't weakened
But it has been altered
Focused on self-protection and satisfaction
My redwood branches are now shorter, but stronger
Growing and flourishing in the direction of the sun
My muscular essence still intact

Sylvie

"It's as simple as that… I just enjoy sex."
—Vachon

"Mmm. Mmm. Shit. *Oh!* Fuck me! Fuck me! Your dick is Goliath… mmm… *oh!*" Sylvie erupted.

"You like that? You like how I fuck you?" he asked.

"You know just how to make my pussy talk."

"Oh!" he moaned as he came deep inside her.

Moments later Sylvie rolled over, looking for her panties. "I gotta get going. I promised the ladies I would meet them for lunch. She quickly exited the bed and made her way to the bathroom to shower.

"The money is there. I sent it," exclaimed the naked gentleman, who remained stretched across the bed, while Sylvie was still in the bathroom.

"Thanks. I hope to see you again soon. That was fun," she replied, as she departed the bathroom with her bags in tow.

It was a beautiful, sunny, warm day, and the ladies thought it would be nice to meet at a local café along the California coastline for an outdoor meal to discuss the "who's," the "now what's," and the "what the hell's." They were old high school classmates and had remained Sylvie's closest confidants over the last 15 years.

Sylvie and her high school girlfriends had traditionally met weekly to consort. It was their way of maintaining the friendship.

The ladies greeted one another with warm hugs before taking their seat at the outdoor table.

"You ladies are looking fabulous, as usual," smiled Carla. "Well…you do look great, Sylvie, and that sundress is so cute, but what's going on with the hair? Looks like you just rolled out of bed. Seriously."

The other ladies giggled and waited for Sylvie to reply.

"Maybe because I *did* just roll out of *a* bed," Sylvie replied, after waiting a moment for the waiter to finish filling their water glasses.

"How long are you going to continue to do this?" asked Becka. "I mean, I don't understand. You're ed-u-ca-ted. You don't have to continue to prostitute yourself."

"First, I'm not a prostitute," whispered Sylvie with tightly pursed lips, as she scanned her peripheral for eavesdroppers. "I'm a paid companion. I accompany these men at events and provide them with a girlfriend-like experience when they need it."

"Sounds like a paid Ho," noted Carla, sarcastically.

"*Well* paid. I make much more money than all you bitches, and I just so happen to enjoy it," said Sylvie irritably.

"Ugh, ho don't say?" joked Becka.

Sylvie glared at Becka and rolled her eyes.

"Look, you're a nutritionist—a good one. When you got into money trouble a few years back, we thought this would be temporary, just to get some of your debt paid, but it's been four years, and you're running around behaving like a high-priced whore. No offense, but Sylvie, you're better than this," said Carla.

"Whatever," said Sylvie, waving her hand dismissively. "I'm hosting an event this weekend for a group of men from a large accounting firm at the Hillcrest Hotel and Spa, and I will make more money in a day than you guys make in a month. So, say what you want; that bachelor's degree in nutrition never paid me like this."

"I'm sure you make a wonderful HO-stess. And the HO-tell is probably the best place for you to *host* it." Said Becka, again jokingly.

"Enough with the ho jokes Becka," Sylvie retorted.

"Ho no like it." giggled Becka.

Sylvie again rolled her eyes. "I will retire from this one day, but for now, I'm enjoying my freedom and having fun."

"Sylvie, Becka, and Carla are right. You're better than this, and we worry about you. Life is more than dollar signs, and we don't want anything HO-rrific to happen to you," snickered Kate. "I know. I'm sorry. I couldn't resist, but all jokes aside, we worry about you."

"I'm not like you all, and I'm done talking about it. Let's just enjoy our lunch and let me hear all the boring shit you guys have done this week."

Over the next few months, Sylvie continued to build her clientele. She serviced wealthy businessmen, politicians, and celebrities. Sylvie kept herself well-dressed and manicured, looking as rich as the men she served. She was beautiful. Born to a Jewish mother, and a father who was of African American and Indian descent, Sylvie looked like a hodge-podge of worlds, blended in the best way. Her lightly tanned, 5'6", slender body complemented any outfit—and any man.

Sorrie McGregor, a middle-aged Hollywood actor well-known for his roles in action films and his recent role in the television drama series "Deadly Games," had heard about Sylvie's highly rated services and sought her out. Sorrie was unmarried and uninvolved in any serious romantic relationships, but he desired the company of a woman physically and intellectually. He negotiated a contract with Sylvie for 30 days. After a battery of medical exams and blood serologies for both Sorrie and Sylvie, she was ready to spend the next few weeks with the renowned celebrity in his home in the California Coastal Mountain area.

The winding drive along the scenic California coast proved to be just as mesmerizing now as it was in Sylvie's first memory of taking the coastal drive with her parents on one of their Sunday afternoon excursions. The contrast between the coastal rocks and the forested hills above yielded a beauty of their own, which was very different from the coastal plains of the South. Sylvie sat in the backseat of the luxury SUV, staring out the window through her black designer shades, marveling at the sights and internally reveling at the life she had fashioned for herself. Her life as a paid companion had enriched her financially and had given her experiences that working solely as a nutritionist would never have afforded her. Sylvie believed that her work provided a service that was an equal benefit to her and her clientele, as well as the community they lived in. Her business thwarted the use of criminal street enterprises, such as pimps and drug dealers, whose ultimate mission was not to provide stellar services, but rather to push drugs and exploit the weaknesses and traumas of vulnerable women and men. No, Sylvie answered to no one other than herself. She closed the deals. She made the rules, and there was deep satisfaction in that.

The SUV meandered its way through hills interspersed with luxury homes, quaint boutiques, and cafés, until they eventually arrived at a large white stucco home perched midway on the hill, landscaped with California lilacs and poppies that were nestled neatly under large sycamore trees. Sylvie admired the modern architectural design and once again reflected on the richness of her life. *Unlimited possibilities.*

Sylvie had not yet met Sorrie in person. Their interactions had been by video conferencing, due to his busy schedule. Nonetheless, Sylvie felt at ease with the agreement to be in his company for an extended period.

The driver assisted Sylvie with her luggage inside the sprawling home, after first being welcomed in by the housekeeper. *Who knew housekeepers still wear uniforms?* As Sylvie peered up at the elaborate iron staircase, Sorrie casually made his way down, as if he were greeting an old acquaintance.

"Sylvie!" exclaimed Sorrie. "It's nice to finally meet you in person. And, uh, wow. Wow! I'm mean, don't get me wrong, you were beautiful on the video calls and in your photos, but, wow, you are just gorgeous." Sorrie cocked his head to the side, lending his thoughts to the manifestation of her beauty.

"Let me show the room where you will be staying, but I hope you take your girlfriend role seriously and reside with me in my room most of the time."

Sylvie gave Sorrie a seductive grin and followed him to her bedroom. She left her bags unpacked on the floor, to be situated later, so she could finish the home tour with him. As they walked out of the modestly decorated room, a young woman, scantily dressed in a mid-top and shorts so short that the crest of her buttocks spilled out from the bottom, walked up next to them. She was tall, thin and had a cheerleader presence about her.

"Sylvie, this is Brit. Brit will be staying here, as well, as a kind of supplement for you. I hope you ladies don't mind working together. Oh, and Sylvie—just so you know, Brit has had all her lab tests done as recently as yesterday. They're all negative, and I can hand over a copy to you," said Sorrie pointedly.

Sylvie was caught off guard. She hadn't planned on sharing her time with another woman, but she was relieved that he ensured Brit was tested, and that it wouldn't change the contractual agreement. "Nice to meet you,' said Sylvie. "I guess we'll get to know each other more over these next few weeks."

Brit smiled, "Sure." And she continued her way down the hall.

Over the next few days, Sylvie became Sorrie's girlfriend as planned, accompanying him to late-night dinners, fun outings, and simple lounging at home. Brit was more like the "side chick," but somehow, it worked. Sorrie often cozied up to Sylvie, conversing with her about the most clandestine details of his life without trepidation, as Sylvie had already signed an NDA. Sylvie gleamed at the sudden realization that her presence with Sorrie was to emulate a life that he could not sustain, while fostering a therapeutic platform to confront past traumas, and some of life's other realities. Each night, she slept nestled next to Sorrie and engaged with him sexually. Sorrie was surprisingly good in bed—much better than average, which was what Sylvie was expecting. No, Sorrie luxuriated in erotic play—especially bondage. Bondage satisfied Sorrie's innate desire to display his masculine prowess and equally submissive femininity; his regalness manifested through sensual torture, and his muses were subservient to his beastly eroticism.

Sylvie, along with Sorrie and Brit, removed their silk robes upon entering the dungeon, which was once a spare bedroom. Heavy metal music vibrated faintly in the dimly lit room, which smelled of sweet, erotic musk. Sorrie had equipped the dungeon with ceiling harnesses, and he systematically arranged various toys and gear on metal hooks along the wall. The evening before, Sorrie had gifted each woman with a guise. Sylvie received a pair of gloves, open-ass spanking panties, nipple covers, and a collar with a chain. Brit received a body harness, nipple clamps with a chain, and a mask. Sorrie fitted himself in a body harness and an open mouth hood.

Using the whip in his hand, Sorrie silently directed each woman to a specified place and then had her kneel. Once they were on their knees, he then directed their stance to the side wall, where a large-framed canvas read:

> *You shall only say these words in this room:*
> *Red, Yellow, Green*
> *"RED" = Stop now and check on me!*
> *"YELLOW" = Go slow and take it easy please!*
> *"GREEN" = Full steam ahead; we're good to go.*

Sorrie pointed to the board of rules. "What say ye?" he asked in a deep, dark tone.

Sylvie, "Green."

Brit, "Green."

Sorrie inaudibly circled slowly around Sylvie and Brit, spanking them with the whip and running the whip gently down their backs and between their legs. Sylvie was aroused. On all fours, she began to move her torso and hips in circles, tightening and releasing her inner loins and moaning in ecstasy with every slap of the whip. Sorrie reached around, grabbed Sylvie by her chain, pulled her collared neck back, and spanked her repeatedly. For Sylvie, this pain was not a show of brutality, but rather an enticing act of docility that was uncharacteristically dissimilar to her natural self, and she revealed in her alter ego. Brit, still on her knees, looked on as her body ignited with sexual excitement.

Sorrie slapped Sylvie on her supple, round ass, gripped her neck chain, spanked her, and told her to crawl, as if he were a jockey, and Sylvie were an obedient horse. Sorrie jockeyed Sylvie until she rested in front of Brit, who had now positioned herself in a birthing position, seated upright, resting on her hands, with her legs perched like two mountains with a forested gully nestled in between. Sorrie yanked Sylvie's collared chain with rigid force until her neck crested, and she let out an audible breath. He then penetrated her from behind with a lubricated dildo, slowly repeating the motion in her silky, warm nucleus. Sylvie moaned, and her head was positioned between Brit's thighs. Brit could feel Sylvie's warm breath on her inner thighs, creating a clitoral vibration that percolated a river of sweetness that crested on her swollen lips. Sorrie was also aroused. His stick became engorged and stiffer than the branches of a Sycamore tree. Watching the wetness pool around Brit's open thighs enticed him. He ceased his engagement with Sylvie, stepped in front of her, knelt, and forcibly wrapped his arms around Brit's thighs, pulling her in close and plunging his thick sword deep into her pussy. Sylvie reached around Sorrie and tugged on Brit's nipple clamps. For Brit, the pain was so intense and erotic that she began to climax, squirting immensely and flooding the floor underneath her bottom.

Sorrie pulled out once Brit had finished reaching her orgasmic pinnacle, lay on his back, and signaled to Sylvie to mount him—and she did. Sylvie rode him bareback, like a skilled cowgirl, determined to tame a wild horse. While Sylvie was home on the range of Big Dick Sorrie Mountain, Brit lubricated her fingers and inserted one into Sorrie's rectum. Sorrie initially clenched, then relaxed with a deep breath, and the repeated penetration against his prostate caused him to swell even more. Sorrie couldn't control it any longer. He erupted deep inside Sylvie. With his hard dick rubbing against her g-spot, Sylvie uncontrollably throbbed, fully releasing her creamy dam.

Although the night before was long and intense, neither of the three were accustomed to sleeping in. In a sports bra and leggings, ready for her morning coffee, and then a long run in the brisk open air, Sylvie walked into the downstairs kitchen and observed Brit seated at the small round wooden table, nursing a smoothie, and Sorrie standing motionless, keenly watching the small TV screen nestled in the corner of the room and holding his coffee. As she made her way to the coffeemaker, Sylvie greeted Brit with a quick rub on her back and witnessed the dark skies through the west-facing window. The Santa Ana winds were howling through the sky, making their presence known. Sylvie brewed her cup of joe and stood next to Sorrie, curious to learn about the news story that was capturing his attention.

The news anchor explained, *"We are now getting reports that more fires are continuing to spread through the Pacific Palisades community. Local fire and police responders have begun to evacuate certain areas; however, residents are reporting that homes were up in flames before they were given an evacuation notice. Many of the residents are reporting that they only had moments to leave before witnessing their home being engulfed in flames. Wind gusts are being measured between 20 and 60 miles per hour, and it does not appear that any of the blazes are contained at this moment."*

"Fires are not new to this area, nor are the Santa Ana winds. Looks like there's just smoke from nearby fires. If they're five miles away, then we'll be fine. The fire crew will put them out quickly," Sylvie said. "Right?" After no response from Sorrie, Sylvie looked to her side and found that Sorrie was gone. "Sorrie! Sorrie!" Sylvie walked up to the window. "Oh, shit!"

The property below, two doors down, was swallowed by red glowing embers nearly tickling the sky.

"Brit, where did Sorrie go? Fuck!"

Brit shook her head in confusion. "I don't know. He just left the room."

"Get your shit. We have to go. The fires are here. Hurry and we need to find Sorrie. So, grab your shoes and your phone and let's go."

Brit quickly got up. She knew from the urgency in Sylvie's voice there was no time to change out of her silk pajama short set… that had true emphasis on short. Sylvie heard the garage door slam and ran in that direction.

Sorrie.

As Sylvie opened the door leading out to the garage, she found Sorrie wrestling with the keys to his G-wagon and with a small overnight bag on his shoulder.

"Wait Sorrie, Brit is coming!"

Sorrie moved quickly to get in the car. In a panicked tone, he uttered, "I'm sorry Sylvie, I can't be seen with you two. I hope you understand."

"What? No. No. No Sorrie. Don't you fucking dare!"

Sorrie, backed out quickly and raced down the long driveway, leaving Sylvie and Brit standing there stunned.

"Brit, do you know where Sorrie keeps the keys to the other cars?"

"No," replied Brit.

"Fuck! Fuck! "We need to leave. We'll have to leave out on foot and pray someone picks us up!" exclaimed Sylvie.

As they made their way running down the winding driveway, Brit remembered she had left her grandmother's necklace on the nightstand.

"I have to go get it," said Brit.

"We can't go back. We can't. There is no time."

"I have to go back," repeated Brit.

Before Sylvie could usher another word, Brit was sprinting uphill, determined to retrieve the necklace.

The fire was only feet from the side of the driveway, and Sylvie knew she could not wait on Brit's return. Barefoot and barely clothed, Sylvie ran as fast as she could through the thick dark smoke, unaware of the debris underneath her naked soles and the hot cinders that grazed her skin.

Survive. Fuck you, Sorrie.

Sylvie briefly turned and looked back, hoping to see Brit slicing through the hot gray clouds of smoke, but all she saw was Armageddon. She was in a living hell, surrounded by destruction and flames, with not a human in sight. Homes and cars were ablaze along the way. The fiery winds were loud and drowned out the sound of her own voice. Sylvie concluded that she was going to die, yet she was going to keep running until the devil himself encapsulated her.

Sylvie thought she was hallucinating when she saw a fireman waving her down and running towards her. His lips were rapidly moving, but Sylvie could not discern his words, for the crackling flames filled her ears.

"Ma'am! Ma'am!" yelled the fireman.

Sylvie collapsed in his arms once he reached her. Days later she woke up in a hospital bed, unenlightened by her circumstance or how many days she had been there, but once she observed her bandages and felt the rush of pain throughout her skin, she remembered. *Brit. The fire.*

"So, the Ho finally awakens," snickered Becka. "We've been taking turns staying with you here and your mom just left about an hour ago. I'm so glad to see you've finally woken up. You've had us all scared."

"I'm glad I'm waking up to you here and not my mom." "Ugh," groaned Sylvie in discomfort. "I don't want to have to explain any of this to her right now." Sylvie attempted to sit up, grimacing with pain. "There was a young lady staying there with me."

"Brittney Keen."

"Yes. Does anyone know what happened to her?"

"I'm sorry Sylvie," said Becka solemnly. "But they found her floating in the pool. It appears that when the flames surrounded the house, she thought the pool would be safe. Fire swept across it. I'm so sorry."

Sylvie wept. She hadn't known Brit for long, but she liked her. She felt tremendous sorrow for how Brit died.

Damn you Sorrie!

After her recovery, Sylvie started her own nutrition consulting business. Subsequently, Sylvie vowed that she would never go back to escorting, and in just a short time, she had enough clients to generate a decent monthly income. It was still no comparison to her salary as a paid companion, but in so many ways, this job was similar. She was still helping clients achieve something that would allow them to shine in a brighter light or display a better version of themselves.

The phone rang.

"Hi, this is Sylvie McNay."

"Hi," said a gentleman on the other end. "My name is Bo Stallworth. I own Bleekman Imaging. I have a proposition for you if you're interested. $20,000 for five hours of your time."

Sylvie hesitated. "What are the details, Mr. Stallworth?"

Divorced: Lois

"Let me get a medium matcha latte with almond milk and a croissant, please."

"That will be $9.52," said the cashier.

"An almond milk lady. It's nice to see we milk alternative crusaders are still out here representing," snickered the gentlemen standing behind Lois.

Lois pivoted around, solely planning to engage the man behind her with a smirk and a nod, only to find a young, tall handsome gentleman, sporting jogging pants and a crisp t-shirt, and gleaming a sexy smile.

"Yeah, I let go of milk a long time ago. It's better for the environment—and my stomach. Although, I do go for some cookies and cream ice cream every now and then," responded Lois.

"Ahh, no! You have to fully commit."

"Yeah, no. Cookies and cream ice cream needs to be made with real milk. That's the only way."

"By the way, my name is Devin."

"Lois."

"Good to meet you."

Lois returned the greeting with a soft nod and gentle smile.

"I would love to see you again. Maybe we could actually meet for coffee or even have a meal together?" asked Devin.

"Um," sighed Lois. "Um, yeah, okay. Sure."

Lois and Devin exchanged contact information and as she departed the shop Lois thought…

"How old is this guy? He can't be older than 30. I'm 45 and recently divorced with two kids at home. What am I going to do with him and how old does he think I am? And I haven't had sex in so long, I don't even know if this pussy still works. Pussy girl down there, do you still work?"

Lois was giddy on the short drive home. She hadn't been approached by a handsome man—well, truthfully, *any* man—in years. Her children usually accompanied her everywhere, apart from the restroom—well, even then, they would knock on the door, asking for an ETA on when she would be back at her duty station (i.e., the kitchen, the laundry room, or the car). Prior to last year, her small number of social outings were, sadly, often with Chris, her ex-husband, the narcissistic jerk. Lois and Chris were married for 17 years. 17 years of misery. Lois often pondered why she stayed, why she endured a loveless marriage fraught with gaslighting, infidelity, and a disregard for her humanity. Chris belittled her in front of their children and made her feel insignificant. She concluded that divorce was her only option. Lois explained to her closest friends on several occasions that she would rather sleep on a cot in the middle of the Arizona desert than remain living in that home, married to him.

She had a six-month plan. Lois saved every dime she could, until she had enough money to afford a two-bedroom apartment for herself and the girls. Although her marriage to Chris had reached its expiration date and brought on so much pain that the strongest of narcotics couldn't numb it, divorcing him was nevertheless one of the hardest and most terrifying things Lois had ever done. It was a severance that her soul had not prepared for. Amid a dying marriage, Lois could not imagine being in another relationship—or even dating. No, she wanted her soul to know what peace felt like, and she wanted her daughters to see what peace *looked* like.

"I know. Yes, at the coffee shop," said Lois to her friend Darla over the phone.

"What do you have to lose? Besides, it's a coffee date, not a marriage proposal. I say go for it. It's been a year since the divorce was finalized. You deserve to have a little fun. Be a cougar on the prowl. Take him up on it. Who knows? That young thing may be a great fuck buddy. Just saying. Anyhow, I have to run. David's on his way home, and I need to get dinner started."

"Okay," replied Lois. "I will keep you informed. Bye."

Later that same evening, Devin messaged Lois. "It was nice meeting you. I'm sorry I may have come off a little goofy at the coffee house earlier, but I didn't want to miss my opportunity. I saw a beautiful lady, with very nice curves, who obviously cares about what she puts in her body, and I didn't see a ring. I don't know what your schedule looks like, but how about dinner tomorrow or we can do coffee?"

"Actually, dinner tomorrow evening sounds nice. And you didn't come off as goofy, not at all," Lois typed back.

"Good. 6:30pm @ Donald's on Roosevelt and 7th st?" asked Devin.

"See u then," texted Lois.

Thoughts of her upcoming date with Devin consumed Lois's evening. She was excited, anxious, and fearful all at once.

Lois was thick and curvy. Over the years, she discovered that no matter how much she exercised and dieted, her full, round hips were there to stay. She not only accepted her curvaceous physique, but by her early 40s, she loved it. Her hips and ass, she believed, were one of the best things bequeathed to her by her mother, but she thought, *Is Devin truly attracted to this shapely middle-aged woman? What will we talk about? What if, during the middle of the date, he becomes disinterested? Even worse—what if he says he's going to the restroom, but instead leaves me sitting at the table, looking like a pitiful old reject? Oh my gosh, why am I doing this?*

Aside from all the negative thoughts, Lois was set on going on this date. This was her reemergence into the world as a free and confident woman.

Donald's was a mid-scale steak restaurant, where a dress code was implemented. Lois wanted to ensure that she looked young, or young enough, and sexy. Remembering that Devin mentioned her curves in the text, Lois opted for a red, off-the-shoulder, body snugging dress that stopped right below the knee. It was both sexy and semi-casual, and she was hoping it would visually please him.

When Lois walked up to the restaurant, she spied Devin, standing next to the door with a dumbfound look on his face.

"Hey, what's going on?" Lois inquired.

"First, you look amazing, and you *smell* amazing," said Devin. Lois blushed. "Um, okay. This is on me. Really. I did not realize they were closed on Wednesday evenings. I just assumed that all restaurants are open during the week. I'm sorry. I guess that's why there was no answer when I tried to call and make a reservation. I'm so embarrassed."

"Okay," said Lois. "Well, what do we do? Is there another restaurant in walking distance?" she queried.

"Yes, but none are all that good. I have another idea. Let me cook for you." Lois giggled in disbelief. "No, seriously. I don't live too far from here, and I'm not too shabby of a cook… so I've been told. If you're parked in the lot across the street, then you can leave your car there and ride with me." Lois stared at him. "I know it's putting a lot of trust in a man you've just met," noted Devin.

"Um, okay. Okay. Sure—and this meal better be good," Lois said jokingly.

What the fuck, Lois?! You don't even know this man, and you'll risk your life because of a sexy smile and tight ass? God, you could bounce a quarter off it—and those arms… yep, I'm risking it. Hopefully, I'll live to talk about it.

After a brief dash into the grocery store, Devin, in his new GMC truck, drove he and Lois to his home. Devin's nerves were dancing faster than someone with hot coals under their feet, but he internally vowed not to allow Lois to see anything other than a cool and collected demeanor. Lois awakened something he hadn't felt in his spirit in a very long time, and it brought him joy and curiosity. He was eager to learn more about her.

"Is there anything you don't eat or are allergic to?" asked Devin.

"It's a little too late for that since you've already been to the grocery store," giggled Lois, "but no. There's not much I won't eat, and I have no food allergies. I'm curious to see how well you know your way around a kitchen," she noted.

Devin gave a bashful grin that instantly made Lois aware of his humbleness. He unbuttoned the cuffs to his dress shirt, rolled up his sleeves, washed his hands and then put on a full apron that read *"who's yo daddy."*

"Before I get started, a couple of things: Could I offer you a drink? Red wine? White wine? Whiskey? And do you mind '70s and '80s R&B?"

"Red wine will do, and I love '70s and '80s R&B," replied Lois.

Lois sat on the other side of the kitchen island, marveling at the magician performing his great act, while slowly sipping her glass of Montepulciano. Lois had never had a man cook for her, and to do it so elegantly was surprisingly enjoyable. Devin danced about the kitchen like a ballerina and a craftsman rolled into one. Cutting, slicing, dipping, straining, sauteing… and the aroma was rich and flavorful, and the visual was of perfection. Marvin Gaye and Teddy Pendegrass played softly in the background. Lois felt a peace and comfort that she had not experienced with a man in years, and *this* man so happened to be a complete stranger.

"By the way, how old are you?" Lois asked.

"36."

"Oh wow! I pegged you to be a few years younger. I was worried you were going to say you were 29 or something."

"No, 36 and I have one 7-year-old son who lives with his mother but is over here a lot too. And what about you?"

"Well, I am much older than 36. I am actually 45, and I have two daughters," said Lois with apprehension, waiting for Devin to give her a "I better run now" look. Instead, Devin mentioned how wonderful she looked for her age and didn't appear to be even slightly bothered. Thereafter, they humorously engaged in a conversation that brimmed with diverse topics, while he continued to prepare supper.

The room was filled with a savory redolence that would have the most satiated bellies eagerly awaiting to feast again. Devin prepared the table after kindly rejecting Lois's offer to assist. Lois looked on, pleased and quietly excited to break bread with a man she had thus far been enjoying her evening with. The food was plated beautifully: grilled lamb chops, blanched green beans, cheese souffle, creamy chestnut soup, and crème brulee for dessert. It tasted just as lovely as it looked.

Lois and Devin dialogued throughout dinner with ease and sheer delight. The night, filled with amazement, imparted a happiness and joy that Lois had been denied throughout her marriage.

"Oh, Devin," said Lois with a satisfied smile. "This has been the most amazing night. I will admit that I was—well, *am*—truly surprised at how you put all this together. I don't think Donald's would have been this good," she snickered.

Devin gazed at Lois while she spoke. "Thank you," he replied—and there it was. They locked eyes, and there was a magnetic energy that seemingly pulled their souls together. The room went dark. The music was now deafened by the profound electric force that moved between the two of them. Words were expressed through the chemistry they conveyed. Lois knew at that moment that this was more than just a "fuck buddy."

"Would you care to dance with me?" asked Devin.

"Here? In the living room?" questioned Lois.

Devin nodded. He stood from the table and extended his hand to Lois. She stared up at him for a brief second before taking his hand and following him to the carpeted dance floor. He pulled her in. His body was warm. His moves were rhythmic and seductive, and his presence was gentle. Lois felt like a baby in his arms, secure and comforted. They danced slowly through a few songs, and then that magnetic fire pulled their bodies even closer. With his hand firmly on her back, Devin traced the arch of spine until he cupped the back of her neck. With Lois's hair weaved between his fingers, he lowered his head and pulled her closer with one hand cupped around the back of her neck, and the other hand pressing firmly on her lower back, until he met her soft, plump lips. The kiss was passionate, yet simple and sweet. Lois was mystified at how relaxed she felt.

Devin seized Lois's hand and walked her to his bedroom. The room bore the characteristics of its owner: dark, masculine, and sexy, modestly furnished in a minimalist fashion. When they reached the edge of the bed, Devin lowered his head, kissed Lois behind her ear, and, in a whispered breath, he stated, "Let me make your body pulse." He ran his tongue along the side of her neck. He whispered again in her ear, "Let me be at your body's mercy tonight. I want to make you feel good, and I want to put you to sleep."

He clutched the hem of her dress and with a slow intention, pulled it up over her head; Lois stood upright, with all of her curves on full display. Devin brushed his thumb over her lips and then kissed her, meeting his tongue with hers. He fingered the clasp of her bra until it opened and threw it to the floor. Lois remained standing, impregnated with sexual anticipation. For Lois, Devin's presence was bold and welcomed in place of a non-existent sex life that had been emaciated for years prior to her divorce. His lording presence illuminated Lois's dormant eroticism.

Devin unbuttoned his shirt and fully undressed himself, all while keeping his eyes fixed on Lois. He examined her every curve with sexual delight. With his masculine ethos, Devin assertively pushed Lois onto the bed. Lois felt exhilarated, and, without reticence, she relinquished all control. Indeed, Devin planned on holding true to his pledge of pleasing her to the fullest extent. While Lois lay prostrate on the bed, Devin kissed her warmly, beginning at her mouth. He glided his tongue down her neck until he met her breast. His tongue circled around her perky, firm nipples, and he sucked on them until Lois's back arched. His tongue swirled around her body. Devin sat on his knees, held up one of Lois's legs, and very measuredly licked and caressed her ankles, and then went down her inner thigh. He then stretched open both her legs and dipped all the way in; he wanted to taste every inch of her pussy. Devin spread her lips wide to uncover the vaginal bean located right inside her kitty. He his tongue had the prowess of a lion. Lois's pussy swelled and throbbed. She was on the verge on climaxing when Devin entered her. He wanted to prolong her state of ecstasy to heighten her climatic experience. His movements were intense and strong, yet his touch was filled with love. Each stroke was accompanied by sensuality and care. Lois knew that this was more than some wild fuck, like she had read about in one of her romance novels. He was not a fuck buddy; rather, there was something more to this.

Devin would occasionally pull out, kiss her moist cave, and fondle her clit. Lois moaned in delight. Her body shivered, and with one last stroke, Lois's spirit left her body. Her throbbing cat rhythmically pulsated against Devin's hard shaft, causing him to erupt deep inside her silky cave. Lois fell asleep, nestled snuggly in Devin's arms.

Over the next several months, Lois and Devin became entwined and shared a substantial amount of time together.

Their connection quickly evolved and bloomed, like dewy spring flowers fraught with fresh essence. Lois met his son Kyle, and Devin met her daughters. There were even a few times when their children joined them on outings, naively fostering the start of a consanguinity, which provided a wholeness that each of them had subconsciously yearned for. During the times they were apart, they immensely longed for one another, emotionally and physically. One late Saturday evening, after settling down from spending the day with each of their respective children, Lois and Devin were finally given the opportunity to chat.

"How was your day?" asked Devin.

"It was long. We spent most of our day shopping for Tia's perfect dress for her school dance. We watched a movie, got dinner, and bowled a couple of games. I'm showered and in bed. How about you? What did you and Kyle get up to today?"

"He had a basketball tournament… all day! I'm also showered and lying in bed. So, are you in bed and naked, or are you in bed with a sexy nightgown on?"

"Oh, someone is frisky tonight," said Lois. "I have on a nightgown, but I can be panty-less in no time. Are *you* naked?" she asked.

"Yes. Your sexy ass was the first thing one my mind when I got out of the shower. I miss you. I miss touching you. I miss kissing you," said Devin.

"I miss you too," whispered Lois.

"I want you to spread your legs and play with your pussy like I do. Imagine it's my hand sliding up and down on your clit."

Lois rubbed on her clit. Her fingers sliding up and down her wet pussy with her finger barely entering her hole. She moaned.

"You rubbing that big dick of yours?" she asked.

"Yes. And your wet pussy is sliding up and down on this hard dick. I want you to throb on it. Cum all on my dick baby."

"Mmmm," softly moaned Lois. "I want to squirt on you," she breathed. Her hand moved faster against her engorged clit, and she came.

"Oh, yeah. There you go. Put all your juices on this dick baby." Devin came. Lois could hear his audible grunt.

Late one evening, Lois received a call from the hospital. Devin had been in a car crash. *He had them call me first?* Lois, not knowing what to expect, rushed to the emergency room. She was frantic. The nurse couldn't walk her fast enough to the room. Devin, supine on the stretcher, looked fatigued and uncomfortable.

Lois stroked his hand and kissed his forehead. "How are you?" she asked.

"I'll be fine. Two broken ribs and a hell of a whiplash," chuckled Devin.

"Where were you on your way to?" inquired Lois.

Devin delicately reached into his pants pocket and withdrew a small, gleaming diamond ring.

"What's this?" questioned Lois. "I don't understand, Devin."

"Lois, you are my girlfriend, my best friend, and one of God's best soldiers on this Earth." "Ahh," he grimaced while trying to sit up. "I love you, truly, and you are *my* it. Lois, will you spend the rest of your eternity with me?"

Tears tickled the corner of Lois's eyes. "Yes."

Blinded by Love

Pain grips my chest
It burns like hot coal, steady and warm
It spills into a cavern, overflowing with affection
Could this be love?
Could this be what I have been waiting for?
I have seen the lips of passion
And I want to kiss them
But they shy away as fast as lightning
Only to strike me down
Like a blind man standing in the rain
If this is what they mean by
"Love is blind,"
Then I am the blind man
And you are the rain

Tiff and Ben

*"What you chose to ignore in the present will
eventually boomerang to you."*
—Vachon

The cheap, hand-me-down vase shattered when it struck the light blue wall. Flowers, water, and broken pottery were strewn haphazardly amongst the soft green linoleum floor of the tiny hallway. Five-year-old Brody James, in his blue starry pajamas, stood at the end of the hallway, scared and dazed, while peering at the tumultuous scene in front of him. He had awakened nervously to the sound of the shattering vase. Brody had observed his parents' aggressive arguments and fights many times, and in recent months, they had escalated.

"Fuck you!" yelled Tiff. "You're a no-good bastard. You're always trying to control me! I'm not a fucking alcoholic…FUCK YOU!"

"Look, Tiff. You can't be coming in at all times of the night, drunk all the goddamn time! We have a kid, for Christ's sake. *You* have a kid! You're a fucking mom. Act like it. Brody doesn't even get to spend real time with you because you're always drunk," said Ben.

"There you go again. Calling me a bad mom because I had a few drinks. I'm not drunk, you bastard. I'm sick and tired of you always blaming me. *Always!*" screamed Tiff.

"It's two o'clock in the morning. Geez," Ben said exasperated.

Tiff angrily walked over to the table along the hallway, picked up the vase of flowers and threw it as hard as she could at Ben. Ben, wearing his old scruffy blue velvet robe, dodged the vase, by swiftly turning his torso to the right. The vase hit the wall, instead of Ben.

"You've lost your mind, Tiff. You're out of control!"

Tiff lunged at Ben and in her drunken state attempted a long swinging punch and missed. Ben, too, was raging. When Tiff's weak punch didn't land, Ben, with both arms extended, pushed her down to the floor. Tiff's auburn, tousled hair went flying upwards as she descended to the cold floor.

Whimpering. It was Brody, standing there in the hallway. Witness to his parents' violent dysfunction. The air became still. Ben stood motionless, staring at Brody, aware of what he had witnessed… again, and Tiff laid there on the floor, quietly looking away from her son's solemn face.

"Ah, shit," said Ben, while stretching his head to the side, embarrassed. "Brody, I'm sorry, son. Let me put you back in bed. Come on," said Ben, while leaving Tiff lying quietly on the floor in the fetal position.

Ben carried Brody to his small bedroom, down the short hallway, passed their primary bedroom, laid him in his twin-sized bed, and covered Brody with his Buzz Lightyear comforter. Ben ran his hands through his son's hair and kissed him on his forehead before proceeding out the door. Brody, feeling mildly comforted, closed his heavy eyes to fall asleep.

As Ben made his way back to the hallway, he noticed Tiff was still lying there on the floor. So intoxicated, she fell asleep, with a moderate amount of drool puddled next to her open mouth. He nudged her twice with the side of his foot, calling her name in a direct manner.

"Tiff. Tiff. Tiff, goddamn it. Get up!"

Tiff rose slowly and Ben grabbed her arm and supported her elbow, helping her to stand. She swayed a bit, and Ben quietly helped his wife walk to their bedroom and sat her on their bed. Too drunk to take off her own clothes, Ben unbuttoned her stone-washed jeans and pulled them down and over her ankles. Then he raised her arms, pulling her white tank over her head, and using the tank to wipe her face clean.

"I'm sorry," slurred Tiff. "I'm gonna get it together. Be a better wife and mom."

Ben sighed and muttered, "this is getting exhausting. I'm getting exhausted."

Tiff reached out and touched Ben's face softly. Ben could smell the booze on her breath. He loved her. That was the only reason he stayed. He loved her, and he understood the source of her drinking: years of sexual abuse that Tiff had endured as a child from Dina, her young female babysitter, a person her family trusted wholeheartedly. Tiff began to use alcohol at the age of 15 to numb the pain and crush the memories.

Tiff stroked the side of Ben's face and leaned in to gently kiss him. She reached her hand down and began fondling his shaft from outside his pajamas, until it awakened like a wilted plant, freshly watered, and firm like an oak tree. Ben suddenly sank into her softness with unspoken momentary forgiveness. The violence of the last hour was replaced with lustful desire and fiery passion. Ben pulled down his pajama bottoms and removed his white undershirt, grabbed her thighs to pull her closer and spread her legs wide, then he began to make love to his wife. It was the one thing they did well.

That morning, only a few hours later, Ben woke up early to get ready for work and to take Brody to school. Ben had been working as a forklift driver at Dick's Warehouse, an inexpensive home goods store, for the last 6 years. It was not his dream job, but it helped to cover most of the bills. He worked the day shift, since Tiff worked evenings waitressing at Lilly D's, a local restaurant a short way from their home.

"Peanut butter and jelly okay for lunch today, son?" asked Ben. "I've got an apple, some chips, and a few things for snack time, too. How does that sound?"

"Sounds like the same thing I had the other day. Good thing I like peanut butter and jelly, Dad," remarked Brody.

"All right. Now, go grab your shoes and backpack, and let's go," Ben said to his son lovingly.

"Okay, Dad. Is Mom still sleeping?"

"Yes."

"Will she be home later to tuck me into bed?" Brody asked.

"I'm sure she will," remarked Ben.

Ben felt anger and dread. It was 9 PM, and Tiff was still not home. She was scheduled to work from 2 PM to 8 PM. He tried phoning her several times, and each time, it just went to voicemail. Ben reluctantly dialed Lilly D's and asked if his wife was there. Rick, the manager on duty, said she left early, around 5:30 PM, but he also said she left her car in the parking lot.

Around 8:30 PM, Ben put Brody to bed, and after reading him a bedtime story, he assured him that his mom would be in a little later to kiss him goodnight. Ben felt awful getting Brody's hopes up when he knew otherwise. *Where the fuck are you, Tiff?* he thought.

"Everybody Loves Raymond" hummed in the background lowly, as Ben dozed on the living room sofa while awaiting his wife's return home. At 10 pm, Ben heard keys rustling at the entry door. It was taking an abnormal amount of time to unlock the front door, so Ben knew Tiff was drunk again. The door opened, and Tiff fumbled to close it, while attempting to hold her balance, her keys, and her purse. She met Ben's gaze.

"Oh, I'm so fucking tired," said Tiff. "They worked me like a dog today. Where's Brody?"

"I mean…. REALLY?" sarcastically remarked Ben. "Really? We just did this shit last night. Not even 24 hours, Tiff. Fuck," he said, gritting his teeth. "Brody's been up waiting for you. I told him you would be home to tuck him in. Where were you?"

"Come on…. It's only, what, 10 o'clock? It's still early. Hell, Ben, I'm home early and you're still talking shit," said Tiff in a wobbly stance.

Ben walked back over to the sofa and sat down with his face in his hands. He had no further words. Tiff stumbled over to him on the sofa, while trying to kick off her cowgirl boots. "You gotta give it to me. I haven't been home this early in a long time. I'm trying. This is good, right?"

"I don't want to do this no more. I'm tired. I think after tomorrow, you need to leave."

Tiff became irate. "So, you want me to fucking leave? To leave my kid? Where am I going to go, huh? Where do you think I should go? I'm not fucking leaving!"

While seated next to Ben, Tiff balled up her fists and hit Ben on his back and in the back of his head, yelling, "I hate you!" Ben reached over to the side and grabbed her wrists and held her down until she calmed.

"I'm sorry. I'm sorry," said Tiff tearfully. Tears flowed from her mascara smeared eyes. "I'm sorry. Just one more chance."

She reached up and kissed his lips softly, then rubbed the back of his head where she had just hit him. As customary, Ben succumbed to her. He met her kiss with fervor. He pulled up her plain black work dress, pulled down her panties, and slipped his fingers into her wet cave. It turned him on to see her body respond to his sexual play—even in her drunken state.

Ben pulled his pajama bottoms down to unleash his rock-hard stick. He sat up on the sofa and pulled Tiff on top of him. She rode him slowly. Her head tilted back, feeling every bit of him, while the alcohol swirled mightily in her head. Ben placed his hands on his wife's small hips and moved her rapidly back and forth until he released inside her. Together, they fell asleep there, on the old beige sofa.

Early that next morning, Ben got a call from work. He had to go in for an urgent issue. It was 5am Saturday morning, so Brody was still asleep, and Tiff was in a deep recovery coma on the sofa. Ben covered her with a blanket, rushed out, and left the two of them to rest.

"Mom, Mom," called Brody, while trying to shake his mom awake. Tiff sighed, rolled over, and returned to her heavy slumber. Brody had noticed a stray small dog in their backyard around their pool and was trying to alert his mom. He thought maybe she was too tired and that he shouldn't persist in waking her. Instead, Brody decided to get the stray pup himself. He opened the sliding glass door in the kitchen and dashed out to catch the small dog. As Brody bent down to grasp the dog, he fell into the cold pool. He had only had one swimming lesson and not enough time in the pool to learn how to swim.

Moments later, Tiff felt a cold draft that caused her to awaken. She sat up, dazed, looked back, and noticed the sliding glass door open. "Brody, Brody!" Tiff called. When he didn't respond, Tiff quickly threw the blanket off and ran to the sliding door.

"Oh, shit, shit, shit! Brody!" she screamed. Brody was floating face down in the shallow end of the small kidney-shaped pool. Without hesitation, Tiff jumped into the frigid water fully clothed to pull him out. She laid him on the concrete. Nervous, shaky, and wet, Tiff quickly began chest compressions as best as she could, aware that she'd never had formal CPR lessons. After a few minutes, she left Brody lying on the side of the pool and ran to get her cellphone to dial 911. Tiff couldn't imagine losing her only son, and all her shortcomings as a mother to Brody suddenly played vividly in her head. Tiff followed every instruction that the operator gave her. She needed him to live. Unwaveringly, she continued compressions until the ambulance arrived.

After two shocks, and several more rounds of CPR, Brody had a heartbeat again. They admitted him to the Pediatric ICU at Glenn Oaks Hospital near their home. Ben urgently left work to meet his wife and son at the hospital.

He survived. Brody survived.

After two weeks in the hospital, the doctors discharged Brody, but he was not the same. He didn't have oxygen in his brain for an unknown period, so Brody developed seizures. Sometimes, the seizures were daily, and other times, Brody could go for two or three days without a seizure. Tiff was remorseful and felt she was to blame for her son's accident. *If only I wasn't drunk,* she often thought. Brody's new reality forced Tiff to deal with her own demons. She sought help through AA and began seeing a therapist that a good friend had recommended to her.

Ben took delight in his wife's new sober path. For him, it was the first time they had felt like a family since Brody began walking. He pledged to be her support and would attend AA meetings with her, but occasionally, he missed the spontaneity of make-up sex, and the unconstrained passion that accompanied it. It was this passion that had kept them together for so many years.

"You've been sleeping a lot here lately," Ben pointed out to Tiff.

"Yeah, I think I'm just tired. Trying to manage all of Brody's medical care, school, and my own sobriety—well, it's been a lot."

"Sure you're not pregnant?" asked Ben.

Tiff gave Ben a perplexed look. She hadn't thought of that. She remembered she had a First Response test in their bathroom under the sink and immediately went to retrieve it. Tiff grappled with the unopened box and anxiously pulled her panties down to pee on the stick. Three minutes felt like an hour. She felt hesitantly hopeful that they were pregnant again. Maybe she'd get the girl she'd dreamt of…bows and dresses.

Positive.

Excitedly, Tiff ran back into the living room. "I hope it's a girl this time!" she exclaimed, while holding up the capped stick. Ben looked up, shocked but grinning and full of happiness.

Two months later, a sober Tiff was preparing supper when she began to feel some cramping in her stomach. Tiff thought it was possible that she was just dehydrated and drank a large glass of water. 15 minutes later, the cramps grew more intense. Hunched over, she turned off the stove and quietly made her way to their bathroom, as she didn't want to alarm Ben. Tiff undressed herself and quickly sat on the toilet. There was an uncontrollable need to push. She could feel and hear the large bloody clots being passed into the hollow bowl. The pain was almost unbearable.

"Ben! Ben!" she screamed. Her world, now clouded by an instant torrent of emotions, had shattered.

Ben gathered up Brody and rushed his wife to the nearest hospital. Tiff was bleeding heavily. She sat in the passenger seat of the car, quietly moaning in distress with her eyes closed. When they arrived at Langston University hospital, Ben parked the 2008 Toyota Camry in the dimly lit ambulance bay and ran inside to the emergency room to garner help for his ailing wife. The medical team obtained a stretcher and urgently moved through the wide double doors to retrieve Tiff from the car. Once the team arrived at the vehicle, one person from the team asked Ben, "What's going on with your wife?"

Ben explained anxiously that she was miscarrying their baby, and she was about two and a half months along. The doctors and nurses shifted their eyes back and forth to one another apprehensively. *What is happening?* thought Ben.

"Um, um," said one of the ER doctors. Ben couldn't clearly make out his name tag. "This is a no-abortion state. We don't even have surgical tools for it any longer. We can't help her."

"What?" asked Ben, confused. "My wife's not asking for an abortion! We're not asking for that. What are you talking about?"

"I understand your confusion and fear, but the state governor has banned it. So, the tools we would have to help your wife are outlawed, too, but we're only one hour from the state line. You need to get your wife there—and please don't tell them you were here first. I'm so sorry," said the doctor as he walked away swiftly.

Tiff panicked when she saw Ben walking back to the car. "What's happening?"

Ben explained to Tiff that he needed her to trust him, and he needed to drive as quickly as he could to get her to the hospital at the next state over. Fifty-two minutes later, Tiff, Ben and Brody arrived at Franklin Memorial Hospital, greeted by a small team of doctors and nurses that were notified of their potential arrival. The ER team, along with Dr. Kappor, an OBGYN doctor, urgently ran with a stretcher to the car to get Tiff to the operating room, where they would perform a D&C to stop her bleeding. Ben opened the car door for them and noticed that his pallid and feeble wife was saturated in blood, pooling onto the car floor. As the medical team lifted Tiff from the car to the stretcher, she couldn't be of any physical help.

Visions of the past flashed in front of Tiff like short movie reels playing in mid-air. So much of her life was lived in the confines of her trauma. Prior to her becoming sober, Tiff used sex to validate her worth, hide her sufferings, and imitate love. She felt closest to Ben when they made love, but she now understood that Ben had always loved her despite her misgivings, and that their makeup sex was a dysfunctional display of her pasts hurts. The last several months since Tiff had been sober had become her most cherished moments. She softly smiled at the recollection.

Tiff began to feel like a battery that was slowly dying. She was aware of the state's new abortion laws, but never in a million years did she ever believe it would impact her. *Not now. Dear God. Not now.* She's come so far- changed so much. *Not now.* She, Ben and Brody were finally a happy family. *Not now.* Once on the stretcher, Tiff looked at Ben, reached her hand towards him and exhaled her final breath while young Brody, with his face mounted firmly against the car window, watched in bewilderment.

In Love

I'm in love
So, I thought
I'm in love
Maybe it's lust

I'm in love
But how can I be certain?
Those butterflies
Love or fear?
Or the fear of love?

I'm in love
"For how long?" you say
Maybe for an hour
Or even a day
Maybe for a lifetime
Worlds away

I'm in love
Maybe it is really lust
My body responded
Heaven abounds
Reactive to the motion
Staggered by the sounds

Mesmerized by your eyes

I'm in love
Or is it merely lust?

Matrixed: Stacie

The hot grease in the skillet nearly burnt the skin off Stacie's hand. Despite her exhaustion, she was determined to cook dinner for her husband and kids. Truthfully, she would have been completely satisfied with a glass of wine filled to the brim, and a good read before bed.

Fried chicken wings, French fries, and green beans always seemed to be a crowd pleaser in their home—not to mention it was a simple fix. The conversation at the dinner table was light and easy, and Stacie—who ate very little but nursed the large glass of wine—ogled her family with gratitude and astonishment. She possessed wonderful children who were unique, yet intelligent, gifted—and, foremost, respectful and loving—and she had a husband who made her feel special. Plus, he was just outright sexy.

Cree sat at the dinner table, wearing a white-collared dress shirt, with the sleeves uncuffed and rolled up, and the top two buttons opened. After 10 years of marriage, Stacie still gazed at him lustfully and imagined their rendezvous play with genuine intent to be fulfilled.

As Stacie got up from the dinner table with dirty plates in hand, she nudged Cree on the shoulder and softly uttered in his ear, "I've got something for you tonight."

Cree, trying not to expose him and his wife in front of their children, grinned and replied rhetorically, "you do?" Stacie brushed her finger along the backside of Cree's ear before making her way to the kitchen.

Stacie showered and put on a skimpy teddy, laid waiting across their bed while Cree put their three small children to sleep. Shortly thereafter, Cree walked through the bedroom door and eyed his wife sprawled across the bed-looking seductive and ready to play. He walked over to her, rubbed her thigh, massaged his thick handle through his pants, and then reached down and kissed her on the forehead.

"Honey, you're still as fine and beautiful as the day I first laid eyes on you. I'm going to jump in the shower, so I can get to *all this*," Cree said, while pointing to Stacie.

After his shower, and a dousing of cologne, Cree walked into the bedroom with his johnny at full attention. He stood at the side of the bed, and Stacie crawled to him, rested on her knees, grabbed his erect stick, and stroked it. He caressed her chin, petitioning Stacie to draw him into her mouth. First, she ran her tongue up his shaft, then around its head, before taking him deep into her throat. Then she slurped and sucked until she tasted the clear seepage he released. She could feel the perpetuity of his erectness. "Not yet," she said.

Stacie leaned back on the bed, spread her legs, like the parting of the red sea, so Cree could taste her. She gripped his head and welcomed the tickle from the apex of his tongue on her yoni. Cree ate the juicy peach with sheer pleasure.

"Let me ride you."

Cree silently consented. Stacie mounted him in reverse cowgirl style. She controlled the rhythm and the pace, and Cree pulled her down onto him with every stroke. 20 minutes into her cowgirl's ride, Cree tightly grasped Stacie's hips, pulling her down onto his hard-as-steel dick, and oscillated rapidly until he came deep inside her, bellowing a loud, intense moan. Stacie clenched tight, holding onto her wild bull with everything she had; the tension was intensifying. Her head drifted back, and her hot volcano erupted, spilling its creamy magma. Stacie shifted forward, laid her head on Cree's legs with him still inside her, and closed her eyes.

The next morning, Stacie went to view a home for sale for a potential buyer, bringing along her six-year-old daughter, Kei. Stacie paid close attention to every detail: the neighborhood, the homes on the street, the landscaping, the next-door neighbors, and the home for sale itself. She pulled into the driveway of the large two-story traditional family home, eyeing the brickwork, the paint, and other exterior details that might disclose how well the home had been maintained. Over the years, Stacie had developed a keen eye for residential real estate, which was the primary reason she became one of the top agents in the region. She could spot a quarter-inch shift in the foundation—and the drainage quandary causing the shift—better than many licensed inspectors. Her clients trusted her, and she wanted to deliver top results.

From the exterior, the home was well-maintained. She noticed no signs of foundational issues. The roof appeared to be fairly new, and the landscaping was pristine. It was to Stacie's surprise when she opened the door to the beautiful suburban home—only to find it encumbered with clothes, toys, dirty dishes, and even half-eaten pizza slices on the couch and coffee table. It was downright filthy. The seller's agent had listed the home as unoccupied, but Stacie looked closer at the munched-on pizza slice and suddenly realized that this home was *very much* occupied. After being initially riddled with disgust and irritation at the realtor who would list a home with such a slovenly appearance, Stacie promptly concluded that she and Kei needed to exit quickly before the family returned home.

As Stacie was locking the front door, she observed several cars pulling into the driveway behind her car. A group of rowdy teenage girls and what appeared to be the parents, along with a set of young children, departed the vehicles. Stacie approached the assumed to be parents.

"Hi, I'm sorry. I'm Stacie. I'm a realtor from Gersham Homes. I had scheduled this visit because I have a buyer who might be interested, and I wanted to walk it first. I didn't know you guys were still living in the home. It's listed as unoccupied."

"Hi, I'm Deborah and this is my husband, Kirk. No problem. Sorry, for the wild girls. It's our eldest's birthday. Just turned 16! I'm not sure why our realtor had it listed as unoccupied. May have just been an oversight on her end," replied Deborah.

"Maybe," acknowledged Stacie.

"Well, how did it show? It's a pretty nice home, eh? It's a little messy, but surely anyone with a good eye can see through it. Right?" asked Deborah.

Stacie cocked her head and lifted her brow. She thought how absurd and detached Deborah sounded. "Hmm, yeah. Maybe," Stacie responded.

"And it appears we blocked you in. It will be easier to herd cattle than to get these girls to let you out. If you don't mind,

Kirk and I can give you a lift home, and you can come back later to get your car after the girls head home in maybe three hours from now. Your car will be safe here."

Again, Stacie thought, *detached and delusional,* but it also seemed as if she had little choice. "That's fine. I will have my husband bring me back later. Just text me when they're heading out. I live about 20 minutes from here."

Stacie rode in the front passenger seat, while Deborah fastened herself in the driver's seat. Kei rode in the backseat along with Kirk and their two boys. The oldest boy appeared to be around seven years old and the youngest was definitely a toddler. Kirk placed the toddler in his lap; he, Kei, and the other son sat buckled in the backseats.

"1325 Millway Circle. We should be there in less than 20 minutes," said Stacie, shifting in her seat uncomfortably.

Deborah uploaded the address to the car's navigational system. The expected arrival was 19 minutes. Stacie and Kei sat quietly in the car, staring out the window and counting the minutes until they arrived home, while Kirk seemed preoccupied with trying to make the seven-year-old sit still, and preventing the toddler from having a meltdown. The drive seemed unusually long, and Stacie was growing irritated with Kirk and the boys in the rear. As Stacie looked on, she noticed that the scenery was becoming more rural and forested than the route she was used to, and 19 minutes had already passed.

"Is the GPS correct?" asked Stacie. I don't know this direction. Never been this way," she said while looking out the window curiously.

Stacie looked down at the GPS. The ETA was 15 minutes. Moments later, there were flashing lights from a police car in the rear-view mirror. Deborah pulled over to the side of the road. Stacie was fearful. Deborah didn't appear to be speeding, nor had she conducted any unlawful driving offensives, so Stacie could not conceive why they were being pulled over.

The officer moved towards the car with urgency. His hand gripped the handle of his gun. His body language was aggressive, and once Deborah rolled down the window, Stacie harkened the aggression in his speech as well. Stacie deliberated many a reason as to why they were being pulled over, but none of which gave rise to a true rationale.

"Get out! Get out of the car and put your hands on your head! Slowly, both of you. Leave the kids in the car!" yelled the officer, with his gun fully drawn.

"Sir, I'm sorry. I'm not sure what's…" began Stacie.

But the officer interrupted her. "No ma'am, not you. You're fine. This woman and the gentleman are wanted. Stay put ma'am."

Stacie was immobilized with fear. She attempted to call Cree, but she kept getting a busy signal. She could hear the officer calling for backup several times. They waited. She waited. She looked to the back of the vehicle and could see Deborah and Kirk handcuffed and leaning against the car, but there was another man with them. He was handcuffed and tied up. "Strange," thought Stacie.

The man looked to be of Sub-Saharan African descent. He had a very dark complexion, with short kinky hair, and a very slim body frame. Stacie saw the officer nearly yelling at the man and seemingly becoming frustrated, but the African man was unmoved, ignoring the officer's words. He appeared to be verbalizing something. Stacie rolled the window down to ascertain the verbal exchange between the officer and the unknown man.

"I've asked you several times to be quiet. Shut your fucking mouth!" shouted the officer.

"Eh put we, se come si, du me we. Es someh le monty ve we," said the man in a monotone voice.

Stacie had never heard such a language, but she also saw Deborah and Kirk mouthing similar words. Terror mounted within Stacie. The officer was frantically pacing next to the car, paging for backup, which was proving to be nothing more than a desperate hope. Stacie stepped out and walked towards the back of the vehicle.

"Officer Willams, what is happening? What is taking so long? And what's supposed to happen with their boys? Where are the other officers?" asked Stacie frenetically.

Kei rolled down her window. "Mommy, when do we get to leave?"

The slender African somehow managed to reach close enough to Kei and had a bizarre, wired, looked in his eyes. "You get away from her!" Stacie screamed.

"Good. When we get back to the precinct, we'll document that," said the officer to Stacie in a shifty motion.

"What?" asked Stacie, trying figure out what was happening.

"Ma'am, these people are part of a demonic sex cult involving minors," stated the officer.

"Roll up your window, Kei."

Stacie swiftly returned to the passenger seat, and the three children poured into the front seat as if the back seat were covered in flames. The three handcuffed crazed oddities chanted in unison in a language that would have been unknown to most normal people. Officer Williams noted the changing scenery in the rear. He paced with nail-biting ferocity. The once-forested highway had slowly begun changing into a town. It mirrored the sleepiness and familiarity of Mayberry from "The Andy Griffith Show," but it was staged with citizens dressed in Amish clothing, walking in a zombie-like state. This was not Mayberry, and there was no Barney or Sheriff Andy coming to the rescue. Stacie observed the terror in Officer Williams's eyes. They were alone. There was no cellphone reception or backup force; no, they were alone in a world that was changing before their very eyes.

Stacie jumped over into the driver's seat and mouthed to the officer on the other side of the window, "I'm sorry." She drove off and left Officer Williams standing there, unaided, to survive the peculiar events on his own. Stacie drove as fast as she could, not knowing where she was, or where she was going. She tried multiple times to put in her home address, but the GPS kept saying that she was 19 minutes from a place she'd never seen or known of before. She drove for what felt like 30 minutes, passing zombified people that also appeared to be unusually pleasant.

Stacie did not stop until she came across what seemed to be the border, but she couldn't tell what country it was for. There were several cars in front of her, trying to get clearance to cross through the large metal gates, yet many people were abandoning their cars with whatever personal items and bags they could carry and attempting to cross the border on foot. There were masked dark-skinned guards of a similar nationality of the crazed cult member, and they carried machine guns across their chests. They carefully and precisely inspected every vehicle that was entering their country's gates. Stacie, not comprehending the situation she had just escaped, was too impatient and afraid to wait in line.

Instead, she pulled to the side and abandoned the car to walk across the border.

When Stacie turned to get the kids out of the car, she discovered the boys were gone. Vanished.

Kei quickly jumped out of the car to be at her mother's side.

With Kei clutched at her hip, Stacie nudged her way in line behind an older couple that were noticeably wealthy, as evidenced by the tailored, rich texture of their clothing, and their traditional suburbanite haircuts. The couple appeared to be uneasy, and the woman held her bag tightly to her chest. When the armed and handkerchief-masked guard waved them through, Stacie grabbed Kei's hand, and, with her head facing down, she slipped through the gates, with the older woman as her shield. They moved swiftly, but for one second, Stacie turned to look back. The guards were rummaging determinedly through the baggage of those trying to leave through the gates that led back to the other side. *What are they looking for?* wondered Stacie.

The town was grave in the midst of normalcy. It had the appearance of a typical township, with stores, restaurants, and small homes lining the streets, but as Stacie and Kei moved their way through, Stacie observed young women, naked and wrapped in chains, tethered to brick walls. The foreboding atmosphere imparted a panicked expression on Stacie's face that had become nearly permanent. She moved urgently through the streets, scouring for a safe reprieve for her and Kei. They came upon a small boutique clothing store, where the women inside looked friendly. When the bell above the boutique door chimed, the women inside stared motionless at them. Stacie held Kei close to her, and Kei dug her head into her mother's waist, with one of her eyes barely open to scan the surroundings.

"Auntie?" asked a young woman walking up from the backside of the store.

"Chloe!," exclaimed Stacie. "What are you doing here? Where the hell are we?"

Chloe whispered, "I really don't know. I was driving home one evening… I don't even remember how many days it's been. Two, maybe three. Auntie, these people are weird."

A middle-aged woman approached them with caution. "You need to hide your jewelry now. If they find you with your jewelry, they will confiscate it. Any metals."

"My husband gave me all my jewelry as gifts. What am I supposed to do with them?" asked Stacie, quietly.

"You'll need to figure it out, but get rid of it or hide it," replied the woman.

Stacie leaned over to Chloe. "Where's the bathroom?"

"It's in the back on the left. Follow me."

Stacie and Kei followed Chole to the restroom. "Hand me some toilet paper," Stacie instructed Chloe.

Stacie began taking off her jewelry and wrapping it in the toilet paper, when the room itself began to vibrate softly with a low hum, and the air seemed to decompress and expand repeatedly.

"That's the magnets. Not exactly sure how it works, but that is the reason why you can't walk around outside with your jewelry or any metal. The magnets will pull the jewelry right off you and it will even drag you if it doesn't come off until one of the guards can get to you. It does this about every forty-five minutes," Chloe explained. "I haven't figured out what they do with all the metals, or the naked women. When I came through the gates, one of the women here in the boutique grabbed me and said I would be safe here. I've been here since, sleeping on a mat in the back of the store."

Stacie listened intently, while continuing to wrap all the jewelry. Once she finished, Stacie pulled down her panties and stuffed toilet paper wrapped jewelry as far into her vagina as it would go. "We have to get out of here," said Stacie.

As Stacie, Chloe and Kei left the boutique, a middle-aged, bearded man walked up alongside of them most casually. "Get to the pizza shop. Ask for Carlos. Tell him Y-man sent you. He'll feed you and give you further instructions."

Stacie nodded.

She found the pizza shop just up the road and did just as the man told her to do. After they ate, Carlos signaled Stacie to follow him to the prep area.

Carlos began, "You need to get out quickly. They will have all of you—including your child—working as sex slaves. Those magnets are strong enough to pull out the metal inside of your body and burst your eardrums. They use the metal to sell and make weapons."

"But the women are chained. The chains are metal," said Stacie.

"There's a coating on the metal that's on the chains and outside the buildings. It doesn't respond to the magnets. Anyhow, once the next magnetic wave finishes, you will have exactly seven minutes to get through the gates. After that, the gates lock down, and you don't want to get caught. Move fast, but don't draw attention to yourself."

When the next magnetic wave concluded, Stacie yanked up her niece and daughter and walked hurriedly back towards the gated exit. There were several staircases zigzagging to the gates.

Stacie's heart pounded. Beads of sweat nestled on her forehead. There were screams shattering through the air. Naked, chain-linked women were being dragged through the streets and whipped on their way to undoubtedly daunting places to face unspeakable, merciless offenses.

"Auntie, did you see…?"

"Don't look. Keep your eyes forward. You too Kei," uttered Stacie.

She checked her watch. Six minutes had passed. One minute left. They were moving as fast as they could; young Kei often had to jog to keep pace. The gates were in view. They were open, but Stacie could see the gates slowly beginning to close and could feel the low vibration of the magnet humming, as if it were warming up. There were only a couple of guards at the gate. Stacie knew it was now or never. They had seconds.

"Run!" shouted Stacie.

There were less than two feet before the gate was fully closed. She pushed Kei in through the gate, and then ushered Chloe through. Now there was less than 12 inches before full closure. Stacie wasn't certain she would make it. The guards spotted her and yelled for the other guard closest to the gate to grab her. The gate was tightening around her chest. Kei stood there tearfully, watching, screaming for her mother, and with one last collapse of her breath, Stacie slid through the gate.

Relief.

Stacie expected to return to the forested frenzy that she was in before initially walking through the gates. She needed to find the car. Instead, they found themselves in what looked like an area outside Harvard University in Cambridge, Massachusetts. They breathed a sigh of relief. Familiarity. Safety. This wasn't home for them, but surely, they could navigate themselves back to Virginia. Suddenly, Stacie noticed something odd. The women here gestured like Stepford Wives. Their dresses were crisp. Their hair didn't have a single strand out of place, and they smiled—even when there was nothing seemingly to smile at.

One of the mechanical women approached them. "Hi, you all look lost," she said. She smirked, "and you look like you could use a hot meal and bath. Follow me and I can get you all set up."

"I… we, just need to get home. I need to find somewhere I can rent a car from," said Stacie.

A tall, well-put-together man walked up behind them. "You visiting the area?"

"Not exactly," replied Stacie.

The man—now standing a breath's distance from Stacie—grabbed a lock of her hair, twirled it around his fingers, and sniffed it. Stacie froze, immobile with fear.

"How about you ladies go with Ms. Lydia here and let her get you settled in?" said the man, with a chilling smile on his face.

He stared grimly at Stacie, and began to faintly mutter, "Eh put we, se come si, du me we. Es someh le monty ve we."

Stacie's stomach had slithered up to her throat, and her breath left her. There was a vibration coming from Kei's little crossbody princess purse. Stacie had completely forgotten that she had let Kei have her old phone and was grateful they hadn't gotten caught in the magnetic wave.

"I'm sorry, but we need to leave," Stacie said to the man as she and her trembling hand retrieved the phone from Kei's purse.

"Hello," answered Stacie.

"We've been looking for you for days!" said Robert, Stacie's father.

"Oh my God, Dad! It's so good to hear your voice. I'll tell you about when I see you and I have Chloe here with me."

As they were walking, Stacie spotted a car that looked just like Deborah and Kirk's. The one she abandoned at the gate. She approached the car. "One sec, Dad."

"Is this here car yours?" asked a young woman, who appeared no older than 19.

Stacie looked through the window of the car. She could see her purse still on the seat.

"Yes, it is," said a gleeful Stacie.

The three of them got in the car and drove away. Stacie looked down at Kei's little phone. She had left her dad on hold this entire time.

"Dad? You still there?" asked Stacie.

"We've been looking for you for days!" he exclaimed.

"We've been looking for you for days!" he repeated.

"Dad?" asked Stacie inquisitively.

"We've been……looking…. for you…," he glitched.

"What the hell!" thought Stacie.

The ringing cellphone on the bedside table woke Stacie and Cree from their post-orgasmic slumber. Stacie had fallen asleep in the reverse-cowgirl position, and Cree, lying erect, drooled and beamed with sexual satiety. The wet extracts that seeped during their provocative play had become dry and sticky.

Oh, it was only a dream.

Stacie reached over and answered her phone.

"Morning Dad."

"Daughter, we've been looking for you! Eh put we, se come si, du me we. Es someh le monty ve we."

Short Story Addition: Gilbert

Gilbert sat frustrated in front of his old hand-me-down typewriter, blankly glaring out the window in front him. Balls of crumpled paper imprinted with letters that didn't accurately relay the words or expressions desired by this experienced writer lay strewn across the cold, wooden floor. The typewriter was Gilbert's rabbit's foot. He believed it was the reason that three of his books were *New York Times* bestsellers. It afforded him the ability to think deeply, without the distractions of technology and information that was a click away. Rather, the typewriter forced him to search for words and meanings in the deepest part of his brain. Relying on bound dictionaries and literary research expanded his muscular acumen, so he believed. Yet, the enigmatic typewriter failed to deliver the words that spoke to him within his mind. Gilbert hadn't authored a bestseller in years, and he worried that if he couldn't conjure the right words, then this one wouldn't be, either.

Gilbert sighed in exasperation. He reached down and picked up one of the crumpled papers. He thought, *Maybe I overlooked something. Maybe I'm overthinking this, and one of these pages may actually be worth continuing.* He leaned back in the chair and reread the page.

"No!" he shouted. "No one's going to believe this story! Ugh, silly!"

He crumpled up the paper again, cursed, and then threw it at the window. Gilbert placed a blank sheet of paper in the typewriter. Since he had a self- diagnosis of writer's block that didn't appear to have a cure, Gilbert thought he would amuse himself, but first, he needed to replace the ink ribbon. He searched in the drawer, but there wasn't one in there. Gilbert stood, walked over to the closet, and found an old ribbon cartridge. After replacing the ribbon, Gilbert typed a couple of test words to ensure that the ink hadn't dried. Interestingly, it was the first time he had a cartridge with indigo blue ink. He giggled at the idea of submitting his manuscript in bright blue lettering. For his own amusement—and internally wishing for a breakthrough—Gilbert typed frivolous sentences on the page that were unrelated to the novel he was currently writing.

"The clouds grew to a dark ominous gray. A large stoic man stood at the edge of the drive staring at the writer through the window. He had a foreboding appearance. The writer, with a tight squint, could faintly see a black baton in the man's hand. The man approached the window with wide and slow strides, and a gaze that was fixed on the writer."

"Ah, man!" Gilbert exclaimed. "I may need to write this book instead. Ha!"

When Gilbert raised his head in the middle of a chuckle, there stood a large, stoic man under dark clouds, with a black baton in his hand. In utter disbelief, Gilbert slowly rose from his seat and stared. Like the words he wrote, the man walked towards the window. Fear poured over Gilbert, and his teeth chattered so loudly that it awakened the sleeping cat nestled in the corner.

"It can't be so," Gilbert thought. "If I could write him in this world, I should be able to eliminate him too."

Gilbert sat back down. With his nervous fingers, he typed, *"and he disappeared."* Fraught with fear, Gilbert glanced out the window, and the man was gone. He sunk into the seat, wringing his hands, unsure of what had just happened. There he sat, staring at the typewriter with the indigo blue ink. *What if I'm imagining all this? This can't be.*

He rested his fingers on the typewriter again. There was a long pause before he began to type.

"A 10-foot-tall grizzly bear stood on its hind legs in the front yard, bearing its large, sharp teeth and growling ferociously. A thick man with a long, scruffy beard, clothed like a 1600 A.D. Antarctic explorer, suddenly appeared. The man had his bow drawn, ready to release an arrow into the harrowing beast at any moment."

Gilbert peered out the window. He had done it again. His words in blue ink bore life.

He flung himself out of the chair with a mixture of exhilaration and disbelief.

"Holy crap!" Gilbert shouted, while holding his hands to his head. With all the excitement, Gilbert nearly forgotten that the man and bear didn't belong in this reality.

"Oh, yes, yes, yes!" he said. And he wrote, *"and the man and the bear disappeared."* And once again, his written creations had vanished.

Alacrity swept over him. Gilbert considered many ways to use the magical ink, but the only idea that seemed appropriate was to complete the unfinished novel in indigo blue. He would rest for the night—but first, he would need a helper.

He wrote, "*Betty, a tall, slender young woman, pleasant in appearance, with delicate features, gentle in spirit, and bright enough to assist in complicated matters, appeared at the writer's side, next to the typewriter. Her attire was conservative and manicured. She spoke eloquently. She would be his closest assistant, helping him with daily chores, and any other such needs of his choosing. She might even become his lover, but that would be sorted later.*"

Gilbert felt the presence of someone else in the room and he immediately knew it was Betty. The young woman stood there, first examining her hands, and then scanned the room with curiosity.

"Hello, Betty," greeted Gilbert. "I know you're probably surprised to be here, but you will be my helper. Do you understand what that means?"

"Yes, sir," she said coyly. "I do."

"Good!" replied Gilbert. "Well, now that we have the formalities out of the way, allow me to show you around—and please, make yourself at home."

Gilbert provided Betty with a list of daily chores which included cleaning the entire home, cooking meals, and attending to the cat. However, Betty was prohibited from entering his workspace, except for the occasional times Gilbert made requests for nourishment or errands. Having Betty attend to priorities of the home imparted Gilbert the ability to focus solely on his novel.

The next morning, Gilbert awakened to a bountiful breakfast that Betty had prepared. He was delighted, as it had been a long time since he had eaten so well—and an even longer time since he had been in the company of a woman. Gilbert stuffed the last of his biscuit in his mouth and stood to leave the room. "My dear, I can't wait to see what we're having for lunch," he said blissfully to Betty, while exiting the room. Betty lifted her head halfway and imparted a slight grin.

Gilbert sat at his desk with his hands intertwined behind his head and stared briefly at his typewriter before commencing to type.

He wrote, *"Precipitous ashen clouds blanketed the warm coastal landscape where the fishing marina was thickened with docked boats, wooden bins, and nets full of smelly fish. The marina was noisy. There were many free and enslaved laborers, nearly shoulder to shoulder, toiling through the day to clean, weigh, and pack the fish to prepare them for sale. The overseers cased the area with a cat-o'-nine tails in hand, ready to strike at any moment. They were tall, portly, bald, grey-skinned beasts, with rugged teeth and such repugnant hygiene that the laborers would joke that the fish died from the overseers' smell the moment they were pulled out of the sea. Free and enslaved laborers alike were afraid of the ghastly looking ogres.*

Gilbert looked through the glass window. His home was no longer nestled in a forested lot in Vermont. No—Gilbert had brought the marina to his doorstep. His words on paper, glowing in blue ink, had come alive once again. He dripped with excitement. He raised the office window, so he could hear the sounds of the new land.

Betty knocked on the door.

"Mr. Gilbert," she called.

"Yes, please. Come in," Gilbert replied.

"Something improbable has occurred. The outdoors… it's no longer a forest. We're at the seaside, and there are these *beasts*. Horrible-looking beastly things walking the area!" she gasped.

"Ah, seems there is. We may be here for a bit, so you should try and become familiar with our new home. I do hope you like fish," he remarked.

Over the next several days, Gilbert continued to write, and his written world continued to blossom. On occasion, Gilbert and Betty would walk to the expansive market he had written into the novel, submerging himself into this make-believe domain as a bystander. Gilbert had also begun to be more personal with Betty, employing her not only as his housekeeper and assistant, but also for sensual companionship. Betty was loyal to his requests, but she did not fully understand them.

Gilbert typed, *"The enslaved laborers worked under brute force at the fishing marina and the surrounding clove sugar plantations. Clove sugar was a substance used recreationally—but often addictively—by rich and poor alike, to enjoy its hallucinogenic effects. The overseers whipped the enslaved laborers if they slackened in their labor or got caught stealing fish from one of the nets. They would pace the marinas and surveil the laborers, while snacking on raw fish. It was mystifying to watch them suck the meat off the whole fish, while leaving the entire skeleton intact. They would haphazardly toss them, littering the sandy shore with naked bones lying discretely in the sand, often penetrating bare soles. Indeed, the overseers were brutal, but the fishing masters and plantation owners were like tiny kings who directed such great offenses.*

"Don't do it!" whispered one of the enslaved men. "If the overseer sees you, then he will beat you good."

"I'm starving," murmured another young, enslaved man. "I don't care if the fish is raw; I just need to eat."

"Not here, Deacon!" replied the other man.

"I'm tired and I'm starving. And those round beasts are eating nearly a third of what we put in these containers. Simon, turn your head. It will be just a small bite."

And before the young man could taste the scales on the fish, he felt the sharp, painful sting of the whip on his back. He yelled out in pain and the overseer grabbed his arm and threw him out to sea, as if hurling a small pebble. Simon gasped, and shook so rigorously, that he had difficulty clutching the fish. Fear crept up his spine and he began to feel faint.

The ogre waddled over to Simon and with his breath reeking of raw fish and rotten teeth, he uttered, "don't end up in the sea, belly up, like your friend."

Unlike the fishing commerce, the sugar clove plantations were less filthy but required massive land procurement to cultivate the crops. However, like fishing commerce, free and enslaved laborers worked under atrocious conditions to cultivate wealth for the owners. Owning such a business provided a level of prestige that was often envied by those who did not possess the financial means. Some saved every penny of their earnings so they could also one day afford to own one of these operations, which employed cheap or free labor.

Although he was a three-time *New York Bestselling* author, Gilbert was far from wealthy. He grew curious to know what it would be like to attain such wealth and prestige.

He continued the novel…

"There came along a distinguished writer, who looked to invest in a sugar clove plantation of his own. He desired greater and lasting riches that would craft generational wealth for his descendants. His name was Gilbert."

Unbeknownst to Gilbert, Betty had spied on him while he sat at his desk, when the door was left slightly ajar. She was interested to know what he was writing, and if it had anything to do with his recent odd behavior. Not only was Gilbert meeting with local officials to purchase land to grow clove sugar, but he also fellowshipped with them by drinking the clove sugar concoctions. Betty would watch out the window and see Gilbert swaying and acting belligerent when walking home. On a few occasions, when Gilbert was returning home on foot in his drunken state, Betty overheard him say to the overseers, "Whip them good, sir!" She was appalled by his seeming enjoyment of the brutality imparted upon the laborers.

Some evenings, after gathering with a few local men at a nearby pub, a drunken Gilbert would make his way to Betty's bedroom. Betty understood this to be part of her chores. She lay there quietly, virtually unmoving, and permitted Gilbert the pleasure he sought. Afterwards, Betty would roll over and return to her slumber.

When Gilbert returned home late one evening, he found Betty sitting at his desk typing. She turned to him and asked, "are you the reason why I am here?" And she read to him part of the story he had written.

"Betty, a tall slender young woman, pleasant in appearance with delicate features, gentle in spirit, and bright enough to assist in complicated matters, appeared at the side of the writer with the typewriter."

"Are you the writer, Mr. Gilbert?"

"I'm afraid I am," he replied.

Betty swiveled around in the chair, once again facing the typewriter and positioned her fingers on the keys. As he stood behind her, he read what she had typed in blue ink.

"And the writer, along with the novel he had written in blue ink, had disappeare…"

Gilbert became incensed.

"No!" screamed Gilbert. "I regret that I have allowed you to see such atrocities. Please! I beg of you. Don't!"

Ding!

About the Author

Since I was a young child, books have rescued me from my reality and provided me with knowledge that I did not realize I needed. I never dreamed that I would write stories where romance meets fantasy.

After being married for nearly two decades to the same man, I understand the ebb and flow of marital relationships, and being a single adult for over a decade before marrying him, I also understand the variables of intimacy as a single woman. I realize that sex and intimacy are an integral part of our lives.

My background in nursing and real estate helped cultivate some of these stories, but my admiration for history, fantasy, romance, and sci-fi are displayed in this book. This fictional short story novella encompasses those interests through distinct and captivating tales.

www.ingramcontent.com/pod-product-compliance
Lightning Source LLC
Chambersburg PA
CBHW061106100726
47911CB00012B/413